SPECIAL MESSAGE TO READERS
THE ULVERSCROFT FOUNDATION
(registered UK charity number 264873)

was established in 1972 to provide funds for research, diagnosis and treatment of eye diseases. Examples of major projects funded by the Ulverscroft Foundation are:-

- The Children's Eye Unit at Moorfelds Eye Hospital, London
- The Ulverscroft Children's Eye Unit at Great Ormond Street Hospital for Sick Children
- Funding research into eye diseases and treatment at the Department of Ophthalmology, University of Leicester
- The Ulverscroft Vision Research Group, Institute of Child Health
- Twin operating theatres at the Western Ophthalmic Hospital, London
- The Chair of Ophthalmology at the Royal Australian College of Ophthalmologists

You can help further the work of the Foundation by making a donation or leaving a legacy. Every contribution is gratefully received. If you would like to help support the Foundation or require further information, please contact:

THE ULVERSCROFT FOUNDATION
The Green, Bradgate Road, Anstey
Leicester LE7 7FU, England
Tel: (0116) 236 4325
website: www.ulverscroft-foundation.org.uk

TERRELL L. BOWERS

THE VALERONS — RETRIBUTION!

Complete and Unabridged

LINFORD
Leicester

First published in Great Britain in 2018 by
Robert Hale
an imprint of The Crowood Press
Wiltshire

First Linford Edition
published 2021
by arrangement with The Crowood Press
Wiltshire

A catalogue record for this book is available from the British Library.

ISBN 978–1–4448–4719–2

Published by
Ulverscroft Limited
Anstey, Leicestershire

Printed and bound in Great Britain by
TJ Books Ltd., Padstow, Cornwall

This book is printed on acid-free paper

1

'Gonna be a purty fair herd for market,' Dodge told the first-year cowpuncher.

Lonnie Brinkerhoff had hired on a few weeks after Dodge and Reb took over the Barrett ranch. The two old-timers from the Valeron ranch had been running things for several months and Dodge had overseen the gathering of about a hundred head of steers for the fall roundup. Sitting atop the hill that overlooked the box canyon, the two men surveyed the herd, as the cattle grazed the rich grass of the protected ravine. A couple more days to fatten them up and they would drive the beef to market. The young man had worked hard and learned a lot since hiring on.

'I'm sure thankful you two fellows hired me,' Lonnie said. 'No one would give me a job riding the range until you took a chance on me.'

'You've a good head on your shoulders,' Dodge paid a rare compliment.

'Put a winter season under your belt and you'll be as good as anyone on the ranch.'

'I'm still surprised I got the job,' Lonnie said. 'Max told me you let go two experienced cowhands . . . yet you put me on the payroll with nary a day's experience around cattle.'

'Rex and Dekay worked for and with the crooked pair who tried to steal Miss Barrett's ranch. Me and Reb didn't figure to allow no shenanigans on our watch.' He paused to spit a stream of tobacco. As usual, he didn't have to wipe his lips; he was too much a pro at spitting. 'Them two squatted on their haunches while the ranch owner was poisoned and an innocent lady was being locked up in one of them there asylums for lunatics. Then they aided Robby, the worth-nothing stepson, in stealing cattle from the herd and selling them on the side. The other cowpunchers were ignorant or ignored that the boy and his mother were more crooked than a snake's back. Reb and me didn't want no one working for us who would go along with an underhanded ranch grab like that.'

'You two worked for the Valerons for what — twenty years?'

'More like fifteen,' Dodge clarified. 'The two of us went to war and stayed in uniform until it was over. Tell you straight, boy, you don't bond with kin any more than me and Reb did during that time. We sweated blood together, shared water and blankets when it was dry or freezing. Ain't nothing either of us don't know about the other — I'm speaking of what matters, not family history. You grow to a point where you think alike. We could sit for hours and never say a word; face an upcoming attack and share our fears without worry of the other thinking poorly for the weakness; then celebrate being alive without so much as showing a smile. Nope, two pards don't come no closer than me and Reb.'

'And you both started work for the Valerons when they were first getting started,' Lonnie surmised.

'Yep. We happened along at just the right time. Never regretted hiring on with the three brothers, not for one single day. They took us in like we was kin, and we had the good fortune to watch their family grow and prosper. Reb and me feel like their kids are our nephews and nieces, every last one of them.'

'They obviously trust you like family, giving you this place to run.'

'Won't never lose a dollar of that lady's money, not with Reb doing the books. My pard is as honest as the day is long.'

Lonnie turned in the saddle. 'Say, Dodge, who are — '

But several rifles opened up on the two of them. Lonnie spilled from his saddle as Dodge was stunned by a sudden jolt to his chest. He folded over the saddle, but reacted instinctively, digging his heels into his favorite horse. The animal responded gallantly, darting away from the gunfire, racing out of harm's way.

Bullets whistled past Dodge's head. The horse stumbled — then righted herself and kept on running. Dodge was quickly out of range, hanging on with one hand, while pressing his other against the chest wound. He wasn't sure how bad he was hit, but it took all of his strength to remain in the saddle. With little guidance the mare sped towards the ranch house. Even as it came into view in the distance, he was growing faint.

* * *

Damn those rustlers! he thought. *They for sure kilt young Lonnie. Damn their hides!* Patriarch of the Valeron families, Locke Valeron sat at the head of the table, with his wife, Wanetta at his right-hand side. The only other Valerons still living at home were two of their kids — Jared and Wendy. Nephew Cliff Mason and his adopted daughter, Nessy, had moved in with the family and also joined them at the supper table.

Wendy had been working with her cousin, Martin for the past several months. He had taught her the ins and outs of bookkeeping and accounting for the ranch, as well as the family-owned stores in the town of Valeron. Martin managed the books concerning those businesses, along with the mining, the logging and the produce farms. It kept him very busy, so educating her as an accountant would be a great help.

'Martin tells me you have learned most of the principles of accounting and bookkeeping, Wendy,' Locke praised her efforts, partway through the meal. 'Always knew you had a good head on your shoulders.'

'Better not count on shifting any responsibility to her yet,' Jared warned. 'She's been attracting more admirers than the only mare in a herd of stallions. One day soon, she's liable to run off with one of them smooth-talking suitors.'

'It's to be expected,' Cliff tossed in his opinion. 'After all, she's 'bout as cute as a baby bunny, she's single and she's a Valeron. If she wasn't my cousin, I'd be hot on her heels.'

Wendy snickered. 'If you weren't related to us, you would be as unwelcome as a stray coyote — and we shoot them on sight!'

Everyone laughed, including Cliff.

'Besides, Darcy still has more wooers than I do,' Wendy added, speaking of their twenty-year-old cousin. 'And Tish' — Darcy's sister — 'will be seventeen pretty soon — and she will garner a fair number of courting-minded gents too.'

'I'm only pointing out the facts,' Jared said. 'Reese and Scarlet have joined Brett and Nash as married folks. Wendy and me are all the only unattached loners left in our household.'

'I suspect you'll stay an unattached loner too, Jer,' Wendy teased. 'You won't find a girl while you're gallivanting all over the country following the footsteps of Wyatt.'

'Cousin Wyatt hires out his gun,' Jared declared. 'I'm not of a mind to try and tame a wild town or stop a range war.'

'You manage to get involved in a lot of action all the same.'

Cliff smirked. 'Jared doesn't court girls, he courts trouble. Some people have to look for trouble, but not Jared — trouble always knows where to find him.'

'Daddy,' Nessy spoke up to Cliff. 'You told me Uncle Jared was a hero.'

'Uh, yeah, darlin',' he backtracked, frowning at the little girl's honesty. 'I was just having some fun with him.'

'He's lots of fun,' Nessy agreed enthusiastically. 'Like when he showed me how to shoot his gun.'

Wanetta about choked on a sip of water. When she scowled at Locke, his expression darkened and the appropriate amount of scolding entered his voice.

'Jared! You know better than to let a child shoot your gun!'

'It wasn't loaded,' Jared was instantly defensive. 'Nessy just wanted to see how it worked.'

'It is our intention that Nessy grow up to be a proper young lady!' Wanetta declared.

'A young lady ought to know how to defend herself — like Wendy,' Jared contended, seeking his sister's support as an ally. 'There's still Indian trouble and bandits or rustlers to deal with.'

'She's only eight years old, and not

many troublemakers come right into the yard these days,' Jared's mother contended.

Locke lifted a hand, ready to end the exchange of opinions, but they were suddenly interrupted by Shane entering the room. It was unusual to have anyone — family or not — walk in during mealtime without first knocking. The look on his face was enough that Locke didn't mention his nephew's lack of courtesy. It was obvious something had happened.

Shane carried a piece of paper in his hand, which he marched over and presented to Locke.

'This here message arrived in town a short while ago,' he clarified. 'Skip' — the town's telegrapher — 'knew you'd want to see it right away. I intercepted his town runner as I was coming in from the south pasture.'

Locke studied the page and a grave look of concern entered his aged features. He looked at the family seated at the table and gave them the news.

'This telegram is from Reb and was sent from Denver,' he explained. 'Rustlers hit the Barrett ranch. They killed a young cowpuncher working for them and also shot Dodge. Dodge's horse got him to the house before it dropped over dead. It had been shot as well, but it still got him home.'

'Dodge always had a knack with horses,' Shane spoke up solemnly. 'Taught me everything I know about them.' He shook his head. 'Damn . . . uh,' he remembered there were women and a child present. 'I mean, dirty, lowdown scum — shooting Dodge and killing an innocent horse.'

'And a young cowhand,' Wendy reminded him.

Locke continued: 'Says here, the rustlers stole about fifty head of steers that had been gathered for market. Reb took Dodge to the hospital in Denver. The doctors don't know if they can save him.'

'The cattle thieves can't expect to get away with stealing those steers,' Jared said. 'The double B brand is nearly impossible to alter with a running iron.

Where they gonna sell that many head of stolen beeves?'

'Our immediate concern should be the ranch,' Cliff pointed out. 'Nash's wife' — co-owner of the Barrett ranch — 'is his nurse, and about to become a mother. She can't pack up and return to her spread. Add to that, Reb and Dodge are as close as brothers. You can bet Reb won't leave Dodge's side until he is up and around — providing he survives.'

'I'll gather my gear and head out at first light,' Jared volunteered.

'Count me in,' Shane offered. 'The Indian wranglers can handle the horses.'

'I'd like to go along,' Cliff joined in. 'Tish can watch Nessy while I'm gone.'

'What about me?' Wendy also piped up. 'Dodge and Reb are as much my uncles as Temple and Udal. I want to help too!'

Locke raised a hand and everyone ceased their chatter. With furrowed brow, he stared hard at the center of the dining table, sorting the options in his head. No one at the table even took a bite — including Nessy. She understood this was all very serious.

After a few seconds of studying on the problems and issues facing the family, Locke lifted his flinty eyes and surveyed those at the table. He also flicked a quick glance at Shane, who had remained standing alongside his chair.

'This is what we'll do,' he outlined. 'I will make the trip to Denver and, until we know if Dodge is going to pull through, assume the job of ramrod at Trina's ranch. Wendy will come along and help with the records, payroll and any other book-work. Jared, you and Shane will try and get a line on the rustlers. Once you locate the vermin, we'll get enough help to deal with them.'

'Locke, dear,' Wanetta said quietly. 'Sketcher is our assistant foreman; he could likely manage the Barrett ranch. That's such a long way, and you are not exactly a spring chicken.'

'Not to worry, Kitten,' he used his pet name for her. 'I might not be a spring chicken, but this old rooster still has enough wind to crow a little. I'll be fine.'

'As you didn't invite me to tag along,' Cliff complained. 'Isn't there anything I can do?'

Nearly everyone at the table replied in unison — 'Take care of Nessy!'

After the stage to Cheyenne, the family took the train to Denver. Arriving in the thriving city, they next boarded another stage for the ride to a trading-post way-station, a mile or so away from the Barrett ranch. One of the people from the ranch was to meet them there with transportation. Everyone was tired of the many hours of travel, when the dusty and bumpy stage suddenly came to a stop.

'Hey, Buck!' a voice called out.

'What're you doing, July?' Buck shouted from atop the stage. 'Get the hell out of the road!'

'Just need a minute of your time,' came the reply. 'You know we don't mean no one any harm.'

'OK, but be quick about it! I got a schedule to keep.'

A face suddenly appeared outside the open window of the coach. It was a young man — unshaven, but he had washed his face recently. As for his clothes, they were dirty, wrinkled, and appeared to have been slept in for a week or more. In his hand was an odd-looking small piece of black pipe. At first glance, it might have passed for a gun.

'Pardon the interruption of your trip, folks,' the man apologized. 'Would you be so kind as to allow me a look inside the coach?'

'What's the meaning of this, young man?' Locke demanded to know, having been sitting by the window on the side of his approach. 'You're no road agent, not with that pitiful fake handgun!'

'Oh, no sir,' he replied contritely, tossing the thing away. 'My friend and I are looking for a shady character who cheated us out of our mine and stole everything we owned.'

'Members of my family are the only ones inside this coach,' Locke told him. 'If you intend a hold-up, I'll let my son deal with you.'

The young man removed his hat, wholly respectful. 'No, sir!' he stated emphatically. 'Like I said, we was just trying to catch that sidewinder before he escaped with all our belongings and our money. We were hoping he was on the stage.'

Jared moved up next to his father and looked out the stage window. He gave the joker a once-over and glanced at the second man, who was a few feet away.

'The tree branch your partner is holding doesn't look much like a rifle barrel,' he said. 'What if Buck had started shooting?'

The fellow ducked his head, obviously ashamed of their behavior. 'What can I tell you, mister? We was desperate. No money, no food, no clothes — no nothing! We walked all day and all night to reach the stage trail. Like I said, we hoped that back-stabbing sidewinder was aboard.' He sighed in defeat. 'But I reckon he took the train and headed south or east. T L and me probably won't never find him.'

'Daddy?' Wendy spoke up to Locke, peering intensely at the man. 'Didn't you say we would have to hire a couple of men for the ranch?'

Her father stared at her as if she were daft. Plus, he knew when she called him 'Daddy' it usually meant trouble! He threw up a quick defense, fearful of what the girl had in mind. 'This fellow stopped the stage with a pretended gun! I don't hire men who . . .'

'Who do what?' Wendy countered before he could finish. 'You heard him. They were left with nothing. The man stole everything they owned.'

'Wendy's right, Pa,' Jared chipped in, a mischievous flicker dancing in his eyes. 'Without Dodge and the young cowboy who was killed, the ranch is two men short. Me and Shane sure won't have time for helping with the cattle.'

Locke frowned at being targeted by both of his children. Instead of debating the issue, he turned to the man outside the coach window.

'How about it, sonny?' he asked gruffly.

'Do you know which end of a cow the tail belongs on?'

'Yes, sir,' he answered quickly. 'I used to milk cows to earn my keep — been swatted a good many times by a cow's tail.'

'I'm speaking of beef,' Locke specified. 'You know, the kind that is served up on a plate when you order a steak at a café or restaurant.'

The man laughed. 'I reckon I know what you're talking about, mister. And I'll be the first to admit that me and T L don't know a whole lot about tending cattle. But we're both honest as the day is long and hard workers. We learn real fast too.'

Locke skewed his expression and glared at his daughter. Wendy didn't flinch, but continued to show a keen interest in the inept stage-stopper. He knew full well if he didn't give these two clowns a chance Wendy would hound him mercilessly. It didn't help to have Jared also enjoying the situation.

'Reckon they must have someone left

at the ranch who can show them the ropes,' Shane offered up another positive opinion. 'Could be several weeks before Dodge is back in the saddle, so they are sure to be short-handed.'

Locke threw his hands in the air. 'Fine!' he surrendered. Then looking at the man outside the coach, 'If you two would like to try your hand at punching cattle, I'll give you a chance. Wage is thirty dollars a month and chuck for a green beginner.'

'You got yourself two eager new hires!' the man said excitedly. Then he turned to his friend and shouted. 'T L! You ride up next to Buck. It looks fairly crowded in the coach.'

'Where we going?' T L wanted to know.

'We just been offered jobs. Get aboard.'

'You got it, July!' his pal shouted gleefully. 'Mayhaps we won't starve after all!'

2

Singeon Pegg had the family's Dearborn parked and waiting when the train arrived. He hurried forward along the platform to greet his parents and collect their luggage. It took but a few minutes before his mother was seated in the back seat, bundled up for the morning chill. His father, Bingham, sat alongside him in the front seat.

Few words were spoken between the three of them until Singeon had the stout mare moving at a steady pace outside of town. Finally, he looked at his father. The haggard features reminded him of a sculpture he had seen once. If ever a person didn't show emotion, it was the man who had raised him. Stolid and dependable, Bingham was a man of few words and sound convictions.

'The doctor says it isn't tuberculosis,' Bingham finally spoke. 'You and I don't have to fear contracting a disease or anything from Mother.' He always referred to his wife as Mother, due to the rearing of their children.

'That's a relief,' Singeon said. 'Not that I was concerned about you and me catching it — more that it isn't a death sentence for Ma. Did they find out what it is?'

'He said it was linked to the change-of-life stage women go through.' He lowered his voice to a whisper, 'The doctor said the medical term is menopause.'

'Never heard anything about it, Pa. What's it mean?'

'Most women go through it in their later years, forty to fifty years of age. Your mother thought she had been through this some time back, but the doctor says its effects can trouble some women for several years.'

'Then it's a natural thing,' Singeon deduced, not hiding his relief. 'She will get through it all right. The night sweats, the aches and pains, the trouble sleeping, the way she gets anxious or feeling low.'

'Doctor said it was normal for a small

percentage of women her age. He gave her a bottle of laudanum and suggested she take a few drops at night to help her sleep, or whenever the pain or discomfort is more than she can manage.'

'How come the doctors here in Denver couldn't determine her complaints?'

'There are concerns about other fancy-named ailments that only a few major hospitals can test for. Plus, there are a limited number of doctors in the country who study problems of the aged, specially females. We had to talk to one of them there specialists, because we wanted to play this safe.'

'Darn right!' Singeon exclaimed. 'No amount of money is worth risking Mother's life.'

Bingham cast a curious look at his son. 'I'm still at a loss as to how you managed to cover this expense. In the five years I ran the slaughterhouse, I barely made enough to keep the operation going. You paid for the train tickets, the doctors, every expense.' He displayed a worried mien. 'You didn't take a loan against the business?'

Singeon gave a callous wave of his hand. 'Not to worry, Pa. I still live at home. I haven't found a woman who can stand the smell of blood, and I limit my gambling and fun in town.'

'Even so, you've paid workmen to add two rooms to our house, you've built the additions on at the slaughterhouse, and you have at least four men working for you full time, plus a night watchman. I had to cut every corner to afford the two or three people I hired.'

'City is growing,' Singeon said dismissively. 'We've got nearby mines in operation, and with the Indian wars over, there's farmers and ranchers starting up all the way to the Kansas prairie. The train has also added a great many travelers and bought in many new businesses. And now with the invention of cold-storage rail cars, I can send beef to other towns down the line.'

'Even so, I could barely compete with all of the smaller butcher shops in town. I'm amazed at the amount of business you are doing.'

'Timing is all it has been, Father. I took over about the time the boom started.'

'I have to admit, I thought you would call on me to help. You know, it would have saved you hiring one of those men. I can still cut and package meat.'

'Not with your bum shoulder,' Singeon told him. 'I don't want you suffering from the pain of trying to work with that.'

'I could manage a couple days a week. It's not . . . '

'No, Pa. Ma needs you with her.' Singeon shook his head. 'You've done your duty as my father. It's time for me to do my duty as your son. It's my turn to take care of you both.'

'Well, if you get in a bind, I can still do a solid day's work. Once your mother is feeling good again, I'll be pitching in and lending a hand.'

'Always glad to have you — anytime at all.'

Bingham fell silent and it appeared as if Lajetta had taken a little of her potion . . . she was fast asleep, curled up on the seat cushion with a pillow and blanket.

Never having enjoyed his first name, Singeon went by his last — Pegg. Of course, he hadn't been able to do that until his father turned over the business to him. Minding the trail ahead for ruts, he knew the road was well worn and fairly smooth to the turnoff that led to their house. He didn't push the pace of the mare, preferring not to jar his mother any more than necessary.

As he contemplated the situation, he suffered a measure of guilt. Bingham Pegg was an honest, God-fearing man. His two favorite sons had died when a Cheyenne war party had hit their home. Bingham and Lajetta had been in Denver at the time, bailing their other son — namely him — out of jail. With the older boys to do all of the work, Singeon had been wild and carefree. He had been nothing but trouble. He vividly remembered returning home to find Marshal and Huggington's stripped and mutilated bodies. Twelve years had passed and the vision of his brothers still haunted his dreams.

He had changed after the attack, guilt-ridden over causing the two boys to be home alone. It prompted him to go to work with his father and learn the trade. The difference was, Singeon wasn't satisfied to scratch out a meager living. He wanted to get rich, to rebuild the house and the business, to have a pile of money in the bank, to be successful and make his parents proud. Once he assumed the slaughterhouse, he conspired to gain control of the beef sales. He dealt with whomever he had to, hired unscrupulous men to do his bidding, and was now one of the wealthier people in the valley. It had come at a cost, but he didn't care. Singeon Pegg was somebody; he was important; and he would not relinquish the thriving business he had built.

* * *

The stage-stopper had dusted himself off before climbing into the coach. The only open spot to sit was across from Wendy. He took a seat, visibly as self-conscious as a habitual drunk at a temperance rally. It was difficult to discern his looks, being unshaven for some time, with shaggy, unkempt dark brown hair sticking out from under his hat. He was average in size and build, but his eyes were hazel-colored and . . . quite interesting. The stage was back under way, along a stretch of hard-pan, where the ground was firm and raised much less dust. They had the window coverings pulled aside so the breeze could pass through the interior of the coach, making it almost pleasant.

'So, July,' Wendy opened the conversation, while retrieving pencil and paper from her handbag. 'As I'll be the temporary bookkeeper at the Barrett ranch — that's the Double B ranch — I'll need your background information.'

'Anything you want to know, ma'am.'

'It isn't *ma'am* — it's *Miss* Valeron,' she curtly corrected him.

July's mouth fell open at hearing the name. 'Valeron?'

'Yes, this is my father, Locke Valeron, my brother Jared, and my cousin Shane.'

'Holy socks!' July exclaimed. 'You mean me and T L are going to work for the Valerons?'

'Not exactly,' Wendy replied. Then she explained how Nash Valeron had married Trina Barrett, and Trina had turned the running of the ranch over to Reb and Dodge — two long-time employees and close friends of the Valerons. When finished, she got back to her questions.

'So, what is your date of birth?'

'I ain't rightly sure,' July said.

'Do you know how old you are?'

'In the neighborhood of twenty-three or -four.'

'How about your parents?'

'Same answer,' he said. 'I don't know.'

'You never knew your parents?'

July grew sheepish. 'Not so much. I think my pa went off to fight for the North when the war started. My ma died of fever a few months after that. Being left on my own — I was two or three at the time — I got picked up by a passing gambler and dropped off at an orphan home.'

'And you don't know your parents' names?'

'Don't even know my own name.' He shrugged. 'The nun, Sister Thelma, who ran the home called me Number Six to start with — she didn't have a gift for remembering names. Anyway, best I can remember, a couple years later, she decided I needed a real name and birth date. As I didn't have any idea, I told her I'd like my birthday to be on the Fourth of July.' With a bashful grin, 'You know, 'cause of how everyone always celebrates on that day.'

'So you took our Independence holiday as your birthday.'

'Yep,' he said. 'And that's when she gave me my full name — July Could-be.'

'Could-be?'

He covered his mouth to hide his mirth. 'It's like this,' he explained softly. 'She said picking the month of July was fine, so that would be my first name. As for my date of birth, it *could be* the

Fourth of July. And also my last name *could be* anything at all.'

Even though his story was a sad one, Wendy laughed with him. Odd, but he had shown an air of self-assurance when talking to her father. Yet with a girl. . . .

Obviously shy, making her laugh put the man a bit more at ease. 'Sister Thelma took pity on me and eventually listed my last name as Colby, rather than Could-be,' July finished the story.

'All right,' she said jotting the name in the book. 'July Colby, my given name is Winifred, but I go by Wendy. Winifred is a rather stuffy title for a girl my age, don't you think?'

July gulped at being asked such a personal question. 'I couldn't really say,' he managed a reply. 'Reckon a gal as pretty as you could be called '*Mud-hen Stonebottom*' and you'd still have a line of suitors from here to New York standing at your front door to court you.'

Wendy was unable to stifle a mitigated giggle, before she said: 'You've a very charming way of avoiding a direct answer.'

'I'll say one thing — I'm right pleased to make your acquaintance, Miss Valeron,' July said, unable to meet her sparkling gaze.

She noticed a frown on her father's face — and a devilish smirk on Jared's. Shane was looking out the opposite window, but she knew he was smiling too. She cleared her throat and returned to business.

'You said you have milked cows?'

'Yes, Miss Valeron. There was a dairy a short way from the orphan home. I hired out to help pay for my keep, because Sister Thelma didn't have a lot of money. There were up to eight of us boys — hence the reason she called me Number Six for the first couple years — and two girls. Sister Thelma didn't have any help, other than for a volunteer or two who stopped by once in a while, to manage us ten kids. She was strict, but never give any of us a whupping unless we deserved it.'

'What about your friend, up topside with the stage driver?'

'He ain't had much more luck than me. Fact is, that's what T L stands for — Tough Luck. His last name is Purdy, but he never cottoned to being called Purdy.' He waved a hand and clarified, 'Too much teasing with a name like that.'

'What's his real first name? I'll need it for the payroll.'

'It's Oscar. He never had no father, and his ma was downright peeved over being deserted by a man. She named him Oscar, 'cause she didn't really want him and hated the name.'

'Do you happen to know his age?'

'I'd guess a couple years older than me. Never asked him.'

'Then you haven't been together very long?'

'Five or six years,' he replied. 'We worked on the railroad until they hired a bunch of Chinese for lower wages. Then we bounced around at odd jobs for a time.' He wrinkled his nose. 'Even tended pigs one winter. That's when we decided to go looking for gold. There's quite a bit hereabouts in Colorado.'

'I'm surprised you knew what to look for. I wouldn't have a clue.'

'T L knew a little about it from when he was a kid. He'd worked for some old miner dumping slag and helping him out. We got lucky and hit a little color, but we didn't have any money for special tools to tunnel into the side of the mountain. Wes Breckenridge offered us a stake for one-third ownership, so we joined up as partners. We was doing pretty good until he up and sold the place out from under us.'

'He took everything and left you with nothing?' she asked.

'That's about the size of it. I reckon we had a thousand dollars each invested in the mine — considering the tools, track and ore car we used. The fellow that bought it said he paid five thousand for the deed.' He shook his head, a bitter expression on his face. 'He offered to let us work for him — a dollar a day for a twelve-hour shift.'

July's shoulders drooped. 'We just

couldn't do it, not when it was our mine. T L and me had stowed away a couple hundred each in gold at the mine shack. What with Breckenridge taking it, along with all of our other possessions, we . . . ' He sighed. 'Well, it didn't seem right, sticking around to make some other guy rich.'

'So Breckenridge took your gold too.'

'Us being flat broke gave him a better chance to get away. Call us a couple of saps, Miss Valeron. We were taken in by a professional crook.'

'Trusting people is what honest people do,' Wendy excused their lack of judgment. 'If you are willing to work hard, we'll make cowhands out of you both. Won't be long before you're ready to run your own spread.'

July gave her a serious look. 'Don't know what to say, Miss Valeron. I'm sitting here, 'bout as dirty as I ever been in my life. Reckon I smell a little ripe too. Top that off, we stopped the stage like a couple of bandits. Anyone else would have throwed rocks at us.'

'We try not to judge a person without knowing all the facts,' she said.

'I can see that, I sure can,' July replied.

Wendy smiled with her eyes and jocosely warned him, 'Just make sure you and T L don't make us regret hiring you.'

'No way, Miss Valeron.' He displayed a timid, yet very comely grin. 'You won't regret hiring us. I promise!'

* * *

Don Larson walked into his four-room house — when counting the attic, since it was spacious enough for their two girls. A second bedroom held the three boys. Granted, bunk beds and a cot to either side of the room didn't leave much room for playing when the weather was bad, but he was satisfied to be a good provider for his family. Unfortunately, he was not as happy with his present career choice.

'Hi, Donny!' Gayle greeted him with a bright smile. He was amazed at his wife's spirit. All day caring for five kids — all under the age of ten — yet she never failed to run to him and hug or kiss him.

'Hey, darlin',' Don offered her his best smile.

It didn't work this time. She had come to embrace him, but stopped and stared at his face. A glimmer of understanding swept over her expression.

'Again?' was the only word she said.

'We've got a holding pen full of beeves,' he told her. 'I didn't get a look at the brand, but Pegg said to expect some long hours for the next two or three weeks.'

'Stolen cattle!' Gayle declared angrily. 'You know that's what they are!'

Don's shoulders sagged under the weight of the truth. 'It's no wonder our butcher shop went under. How can anyone compete against a guy like Pegg who buys beef for pennies on the dollar? He's got Everett to do the killing and skinning, Ingram for the rendering, and I cut and package the meat. We used to buy a half a beef at a time and try to make a living selling chops, steaks and roasts. Even when we got a good price on the beef or pork, we had to charge twice as much as Pegg.'

'And now you work for the man who ran us out of business.' Gayle sighed her disgust. 'Sometimes it's not a very fair world.'

'At least I'm not part of whatever shady dealings he's involved in. He pays me to cut and fill meat orders — that's all I do.'

'Plus, he does allow you to bring home stewing meat and steaks or a roast when you work longer hours. That's a benefit for our family.'

'How were the kids today?' he changed the subject.

'It's much easier with three of them going to Parker's for schooling.'

'It'll have to do until we figure a way to send them to a real school.'

'Doris' — their youngest child — 'informed me she does not want any little brothers, because the older boys are no fun to have around.'

Don grinned. 'Now we've got a three-year-old dictating the size of our family.'

'Yes, I told her it was a good thing Dewayne didn't feel that way, or else she wouldn't have been born.'

'I wish all of the kids had been as mellow as Dewayne,' Don said. 'In all his five years, I don't think he's given us a moment's trouble.'

'No, he was a blessing after his older brothers. They can be a handful at times — Sandra too. She and Jasper think, because they are the oldest, they ought to be able to rule the household. Mike doesn't like that, nor Doris either.'

'I don't envy you, having to ride herd on them every day.'

Gayle laughed. 'I'm their mother, Donny — it's my job.'

'Oftentimes I think I got the better end of our marriage.'

'Oh, yes. Up to your elbows in blood and bones, working ten- or twelve-hour days, surrounded by the smell of death. I'm not volunteering to trade jobs with you.'

Don grew serious again. 'I happened to get a look at the men who brought in the cattle. They are the ones from the Big M ranch. I wonder if they actually work for Pegg.'

Gayle put a hard look on him. 'Do you think you should tell the Denver police? You said those men look like hardened outlaws.'

'I've no proof of anything,' Don said. 'Pegg keeps all of his book-work to himself. All I have are suspicions. Plus, if I open my mouth, there goes the job and our livelihood. If you recall, things were very tight when I had the meat shop.'

'We could always go back to Chicago.'

'And return to one of the major slaughterhouses? No thanks. It took a month before the smell of that place went away. At least I'm in charge of the meat-cutting and packaging, and I'm able to wash and change clothes before I come home. That sweet-smelling soap you picked out even gets rid of the odor on my hands.'

Gayle snuggled in closer and put her arms around Don's neck. 'Whatever we have to do . . . we'll get by. You're a good man, and the Lord watches over them who do what's right.'

Don kissed her, then leaned back and looked into her eyes. 'The Lord already gave me you and the kids. I've got no complaints.'

'Unless you discover you're working for a crook who's buying stolen cattle or something.'

Don bobbed his head. 'We'll stick it out and see what happens. This is the largest number of cattle brought in since I started. Must be fifty head. The other times Big M has showed up, it was only a couple dozen or so. If the number continues to grow . . . '

He didn't have to finish. Both he and his wife knew they would have a hard time getting by without the steady income of this good-paying job. However, right was right, and wrong was wrong. There was no gray area. If he found proof that Pegg was buying rustled cattle, he would have to go to the law.

* * *

Dutch, the Barrett ranch handyman, was the only one there to meet the Valerons upon their arrival. The cook and one of the hands had gone to buy supplies, as Locke's telegraph message had warned the ranch to expect several visitors. Wendy, having been to the Double B previously, knew Dutch. She introduced everyone and Dutch got down to business.

'It's pretty bad,' he told them. 'The bullet hit Dodge right smack betwixt his heart and lung. An inch either way, it would have kilt him sure. The Brinkerhoff kid was hit three times, so we figure he was closest to the shooters. Poor Lonnie, never got to enjoy much of his adult life.'

'How long since you've heard from Reb?' Locke asked.

'Yesterday. He sent a telegraph message to the way station and the owner's kid brought over the wire — along with the second from you saying you would arrive today.' Dutch reached into his shirt pocket and removed a piece of paper. 'You can read what Reb said, but it's just what I've told you.'

Locke looked over Reb's message and sighed. 'I'll take a buggy tomorrow morning and visit them both. My body doesn't react well to horseback riding any more.'

'Whatever you want, Mr Valeron,' Dutch offered. 'I'll have you a team and the most comfortable buggy on the ranch ready and waiting.'

'I hope you have some good riding stock in the corral,' Jared spoke up. 'There's several hours of daylight left. Shane and I need to get on the trail of those stolen cattle.'

'Max is our top hand, after Dodge. He brought in several of the best mounts we have,' Dutch reported to him. 'They are in the corral next to the barn.'

Locke tipped a nod at T L and July. 'These two green cowpokes need most everything. They are new-hires to fill in for the lost young man and Dodge.'

'Max is working about five minutes up the canyon, building a fence for winter pasture,' Dutch informed the group.

Then, speaking to Jared, 'He can show you where we found Lonnie's body, before you send him back to the house to get the new guys lined out.'

'We also need to buy whatever clothes, boots, or the like, these two men need,' Wendy told Dutch. 'I'll keep a tally of expenditures in the daily log and deduct it from their pay.'

'I'll take the two of them into town with me in the morning,' Locke suggested. 'I'll help them gather what they will need for the first month. After that, they can add whatever they need on payday.'

'Much obliged, Mr Valeron,' July said. 'Me and T L will do you the best job we can.'

'I'll saddle us a couple horses, Jer,' Shane told his cousin. 'You get what supplies you can find and we'll get on the trail of those ambushing maggots.'

'Pick an extra one for a pack animal,' Jared replied. 'We'll take extra water and food enough for several days. We've got to make up a lot of time.'

Locke watched as Shane hurried off to get started, then he spoke to his son. 'You know those cattle are long gone by now. No one is going to hang onto fifty head of stolen beef.'

'Pa, if there's a trail, we'll follow it. If it leads us to someone involved, we'll get the information we need to keep after the rustlers. Shane and I won't quit until we track down the varmints who shot Dodge and killed the young cowhand. If it takes us a week, so be it. If it takes a month, we'll still get the job done.'

'Just don't go trying to handle a dozen men by yourself,' Locke warned. 'You find those killers, you get word to us. I'll see you get enough help to do the job.'

'Yeah, Pa,' Jared responded in a pacifying tone of voice. 'I'm not Wyatt. I won't tackle a host of rustlers on my own.'

'Speaking of your cousin, I'll try and track him down. He is very fond of Dodge and Reb too.'

Wendy reached over and took hold of Jared's arm. Rather than her usual wit or sarcasm, she was deadly serious.

'These are cold-blooded killers, Jerry,' she said gravely. 'Be careful . . . and take care of Shane. He's not much of a shot with a gun.'

'I'll send for help when I find those coyotes,' he promised. Then he swung his attention to Dutch. 'You said the cook has gone shopping. How are you fixed for supplies?'

'There's plenty of tins of beans, some jerky, and a pork shoulder hanging in the smokehouse. I believe we've got some air-tights of peaches and plenty of coffee on hand.'

'I'll put together a few days' worth of goods,' Jared said. 'We can buy more as we need it.'

'You have enough money?' Locke wanted to know.

'Depends on how long this takes. I can always wire you and have funds sent to a bank or a Wells Fargo office.'

Locke dug out some money and passed it to him. 'Keep us informed as best you can,' he instructed. 'If you need anything — '

'Yeah, Pa,' Jared grinned. 'I'll keep you posted.'

'I'll help you pack the stuff for your supplies,' Wendy offered. 'I know what a scatterbrain you can be when you get involved in something. You'd likely forget to pack the salt.'

3

Don Larson had scribbled out an order for the butcher's wrap and packaging supplies he needed. With so many beef to process, it was going to be a job to keep up with orders. The cold locker seldom had more than ten to twenty sides of beef at a time, but Pegg hated to spend money feeding the cattle in the holding pen. He would want to move the product as quickly as possible.

As he approached Pegg's office, he overheard voices and stopped. Pegg did not sound happy.

'. . . so many at one time!' his boss was ranting. 'I told you no more than twenty-five!'

A second voice replied. 'For hell sakes, Pegg! You're making a fortune here! Me and the boys need to earn enough to keep us in booze and women!'

'Mantee, you know I have to limit the number of head I butcher this way. I only have my usual outlets in Denver and a few small trading posts to sell to. If you bring me too many head, I end up shipping the meat by rail to buyers further down the track. I make almost nothing when I do that.'

'You're getting the beef at a price no one else can match,' Mantee argued back. 'We're only asking a fair return for our efforts.'

'All right. It's too late to do much else. I'll figure a way to boost my sales for the next few weeks. Gonna be hard as hell for Ingram to render that many head. Bone meal don't move very fast, but at least there's a good market for the tallow.'

'Yeah, it pains me the problems you have,' Mantee sounded off sarcastically, 'making a pile more money than you can spend. When do we get paid?'

'I'll have to withdraw some funds from the bank,' Pegg informed him. 'Are you and the boys maintaining the ranch like I told you?'

'The house ain't much more'n a shack,'

Mantee grumbled. 'Come winter, we're gonna have to cover the walls with cardboard or we'll sure enough freeze our bacon.'

'It's necessary to . . . '

'Yeah, yeah,' Mantee cut Pegg off. 'I know the whys of running our cattle ranch. I'm just warning you that we're gonna have to spend a little money to fix it up.'

'I'll cover the costs,' Pegg said. 'And sit tight — I'll have your money in three days.'

'How about a little advance? Me and the boys — well, it's thirsty work having to nursemaid a bunch of cattle for durn near a week.'

The sound of Pegg opening his desk drawer, followed by the opening of his cash box, came through the closed door. 'I've got two hundred dollars on hand. That ought to keep you in good spirits until I get the rest from the bank.'

Mantee guffawed. 'You bet, Pegg. We can get rooms in town, buy us a couple good meals, lots of liquor, and find a fun-loving gal or two.'

'See you in three days.'

At Pegg's words of dismissal, Don hurried around the corner in the hallway and ducked into the changing room, a place he and the other hired men kept their regular clothes. He didn't see Everett until it was too late to change direction.

'Hey, Ev,' he greeted, continuing over to where he had hung his jacket and the canvas bag that contained his lunch. 'How's it going?'

The man grunted. 'Gonna be busy fer a few days. I'll likely wear out another sledgehammer before the week's end.'

'I don't envy you, having to kill and skin those critters.'

'At least Pegg let me keep the Swedish kid. Hans ain't very big, but he's a workin' fool.'

'Beats the occasional meat-wrapper he hires to help me. I usually spend more time teaching them what to do than they spend doing the job.'

To cover why he had come into the room, Don went through the jacket and pulled out some pieces of wrapped hard-candy.

'Want one?' he asked the burly-built Everett. 'Butterscotch.'

'Naw,' he said. 'I've got bad teeth. They get to aching if I suck on candy or sugar sticks.'

'Ouch!' Don empathized. 'That's gotta be tough.'

'Last time I seen a dentist, he said my teeth would mostly have to be pulled. Said the new replacement teeth were made of some kind of hard rubber, much cheaper than the ivory ones they used to use.'

Don expressed his sympathy again, then changed the subject. 'I've never seen so many cattle at one time. The holding pen looks too crowded for the cattle to even lie down.'

'The boss got a good deal on them.' He snorted. 'You know Pegg — got a nose for a dollar that would beat any hound.'

'Going to mean a lot of work for us.'

Everett nodded. 'Pegg promised he'd get some short-time help. And Ingram has his two cousins to lend a hand with the rendering. I swear, Pegg makes more money from selling the tallow for candles, soap and glue than from the sale of beef.'

'Not a job for me, melting down fat day after day,' Don said. 'It gets hot enough slaving over the cutting table.'

'Try being inside the skinning room,' Everett returned. 'Freeze in winter and bake in the summer.'

Don put a couple of the sweets in his pocket. 'I better get some supplies ordered. Hate to have Pegg climbing my back for not keeping on top of the packaging.'

'Wouldn't trade you or Ingram's jobs,' Everett said, shaking his shaggy mane. 'Nope. Once they's skinned, hung and split, they's not mine to worry about.'

Don gave a nod and went out of the room. He found Pegg behind his desk, spectacles on his nose, scribbling on a pad of paper. *Probably figuring how much money he was going to make from those bargain-priced cattle!* he thought.

'I've got a list of supplies, Pegg. After seeing the full holding pen out back, I hope I've ordered enough.'

The owner looked up from under a pair of bushy eyebrows. 'Supplies, huh? Soon as Louie has the water troughs filled, I'll send him to town. Ingram has a few things he needs too.'

Don passed over the list of items. Pegg glanced over it and gave his approval. 'New saw blades again?' He didn't expect an answer, saying, 'Looks good. I hope I can get enough orders to keep up with you and Everett.'

'You've about got every market covered,' Don commented. 'Every eatery in town, the hospital, the stores — even the local work gangs and the prison are buying from you. And the tallow — that market seems to never run out.'

'That's true enough, but we've got fifty animals this time. It's the most I ever had to deal with at one time. Sure can't afford to feed them grain and hay for weeks at a time.'

'I saw Pierce Mantee leaving just now.

Are these cattle all from his ranch?'

Pegg gave a shrug of indifference. 'It's one of those quick turnovers. He bought the cattle from some little rancher on the Western Slope. The owner quit the business and wanted to get rid of his beef. Mantee got a good deal on them and passed them along to me. Fortunately, Mantee doesn't know squat about the price of beef back east.'

'I don't think I can keep up with Everett and Hans. Any chance of the Gallegos woman lending a hand? She can't cut meat for shucks, but she's pretty good at wrapping.'

'I'll tell Louie to stop by her place. I figured you would need some help with this many critters. My father will also come in to work a few days.'

'Oh? I've never met Bingham. I remember you saying it was him who started this place years ago.'

'He retired when my mother started feeling poorly, but we have an elderly spinster close by who can watch my mother and help around the house. My pa can still cut meat and wrap, although it would only be four or five hours a day. His shoulders get to hurting if he over-does it.'

'Yeah, chopping and cutting is tough on a person's arms and shoulders.'

'I'll get you another helper or two if we get backed up,' Pegg promised. 'And I can also lend a hand whenever I get the time.'

Don thanked him and left the office. He had work to do, getting prepared for the first slab of beef he would carry in from the meat locker. One meat-cutter could not keep up when several beeves were going into the locker each day. He was in for some long days, even with a couple helpers.

Stopping at his work table, he saw Pegg had posted the day's orders . . . and there was already enough to keep four men busy.

* * *

The widow, who insisted on being called Mildred, or Milly, had been hired when Trina Barrett had been confined at the lunatic asylum. She had stayed on when Reb and Dodge took over and was an able cook and good housekeeper. With no one close by in her life, she had a downstairs room in the main house. Fortunately, Mildred was one of those rare types who simply loved to cook and be useful. She put out a meal for the hired hands at daylight in the summer and six o'clock when the season changed. For the household, she often served the same food, but an hour later. With guests in the house, she enjoyed showing off her culinary talents.

The second morning, Wendy rose to the delicious smell of flapjacks, eggs and bacon. She was about to sit down to the table when she saw July Colby ride in. She mentioned it to Dutch, who usually ate with the hired help.

'Unlucky stiff,' he grinned without humor. 'He drew the night watch. Max is breaking them new boys in right. Give um a taste of cattle-tending right off, so they know this is a real job.'

'Then he didn't get here in time to eat breakfast,' she determined.

'Mildred will rustle him up a little something.'

But Wendy was already going to the door. She waved to July, who neck-reined his horse over to the front porch.

'Sit yourself down in one of the chairs here on the porch,' she told him. 'I'll bring you out a plate of food.'

'You don't have to do that, Miss Valeron,' July protested. 'Max said I could . . . '

'My father happens to be ramrodding this ranch at the moment,' Wendy cut him off curtly. 'I expect you to do what you're told.'

The words were delivered with a degree of humor, rather than an outright demand. July tipped his hat and displayed a good-natured grin.

'Proud to do your bidding, Miss Valeron,' he said, his eyes showing amusement of his own. 'I'll tie off my steed and park myself in a chair.'

Wendy returned to the table and quickly made up two plates. She didn't manage her escape quick enough. Her father entered the room and shot her a curious glance.

'What're you up to, daughter?'

'Um . . . just promoting a little goodwill between employer and employee,' she replied flippantly. 'Excuse me for not eating at the table with you this morning.'

Locke flicked his eyes to the man on the porch. He saw July was brushing the dust off of his clothes and smoothing out his freshly groomed hair at the same time.

'I'd mention something about the status of being a Valeron and my desires for future suitor prospects,' he grunted sourly, 'but I'm sure it would be a waste of breath.'

Wendy lifted her chin as if to begin a lecture. 'I remember you telling me once — '*Winifred, there's one thing I want you to always remember — regardless of wealth or social position, you are no better than anyone else — but you are darn well as good!'*'

'I believe another quote comes to mind — how something a man says without thinking first can come back to bite him on the rump!'

She laughed and picked up the two plates. Locke, rather than disputing what she was up to, moved quickly over and opened the door for her.

Wendy balanced the two plates, having a cup of coffee pinned between her elbow and ribs. July immediately jumped up to take the cup and one plate of food.

'Holy socks!' he said. 'I ain't had pancakes since . . . ' He shrugged. 'Well, it's been a long time, I can tell you.'

'I hope I put enough butter and syrup on for your taste.'

'Miss Valeron, I don't reckon you could do anything I would object to. This is a pleasure I might have dreamed of, but never really expected to come true.'

'It's just a meal,' she replied.

'But you're the one doing the serving,'

he countered. 'I always figured to have me some flapjacks one day.'

She smiled at his compliment and turned around to sit. July couldn't very well hold her chair for her, but he did wait until she had sat down before he joined her. They both put their plates on their laps and began to eat.

'Mildred really does know how to fix a meal!' Wendy praised, after taking her first bite. 'Have you met her? She's the widow who cooks and cleans here at the house. I had no idea she was such a good cook.'

'I've yet to speak to the woman, but eggs, bacon, and pancakes,' July said, licking his lips. 'I'd guess she's gonna be one of my favorite people on the ranch.'

After a few bites, July spoke again. 'I'd like to say how beholden to you me and my partner are again, Miss Valeron. You and your pa have saved a couple of souls from becoming wayward beggars. I don't know how me and T L can ever thank you.'

'Just do a good job here for Reb and

Dodge.'

'Speaking of the owners of this here ranch,' July said between bites. 'What's the story about the third owner? Max said it is a woman who's now married to one of your kin?'

'My brother, Nash,' Wendy informed him. Then she gave the short history of how her family had come to the aid of the young woman. She finished with, 'Trina took over the nursing job I had intended to undertake for my brother. It was a simple choice for me, once I admitted I couldn't stand the sight of blood.'

'I admit, I'm not all that fond of blood either,' July said. Then he observed, 'As for your brother, Jared, there seems a strong bond between you two. I mean, more than just being related.'

'Jerry has always been my favorite brother. He teases me mercilessly, but I've learned to give as good as I get. Nevertheless, growing up as we did with four older brothers, he was the one who always watched out for me and Scarlet — she's my older sister. If you were to ask her, she'd tell you the same thing, Jer is the one who always kept a special eye on us. He isn't the most kind or gentlemanly, or the best-looking of my brothers, but he's the one who always saw to our safety and needs.'

'You must be worried, what with him tracking a bunch of murdering rustlers.'

She gave a nod to his statement. 'Yes, but I trust him to call for help if he needs it. Jerry is an exceptional hunter and tracker, but he knows his limitations. He has a quick-fire temper, but he always manages to control the impulse when it comes to a fight.'

'Wish he'd have let me tag along with him and your cousin. Me and T L ain't done much fighting, but we sure owe your family a debt.'

Wendy paused to study the man at her side. He was much more presentable, smooth-shaven, his hair neatly trimmed; a little dusty, with tired eyes from being up all night, but there was something about him she liked.

July ducked away from a return gaze

as if embarrassed. He obviously lacked experience with young ladies, though he had not concealed his interest in her. She knew if they were to have a barn dance nearby, he would be first in line to swing her about on the straw-covered floor.

July waited a moment, but when Wendy didn't say anything more, he said: 'I didn't get to talk to anyone but Max yesterday. Soon as your pa bought us the gear we needed and paid for us to get shaves and haircuts, he sent me and T L back so we could get to work. How is the wounded fellow doing?'

She blinked to remove her girlish reverie and returned to the present. Clearing her throat quietly, she summoned forth her mental faculties.

'Father said the doctor was quite confident Dodge would recover. The major concern is infection. If he gets through the next few days, he should be back at the ranch in a couple weeks.'

'I reckon it ain't my business, but does that mean you'll be leaving?'

The disheartened tone in his voice

confirmed her suspicions . . . July was smitten. Somehow, that notion caused a sudden increase in her heart rate and the early morning sun felt much warmer.

'July,' she said carefully, 'would you do something for me? It's not a criticism or anything like that, just something I wish you would try and do.'

'Anything at all, Miss Valeron.'

'Well, Father is . . . um, let's call it *cognizant* of a person's countenance. Do you know that word?'

'Which one — the cog-a-zant or the count-whatever?'

'How about decorum?'

His face skewed to display puzzlement. 'How about you say what it is in plain English? I ain't gonna take offense.'

'That's the word — *ain't*,' Wendy explained, deciding there was no tactful way to present the request. 'You see, my father is one who believes all children should learn proper speech and etiquette. It isn't so much so they can rub shoulders with snobs or people who are better educated. It is for the comfort a person gets from knowing they are able to converse without fear of sounding or feeling inferior.'

For all her careful wording and tact, July simply laughed. 'Oh! Is that all it is?' He continued to smile. 'Sister Thelma pounded those things in our heads all the time. 'You don't say *don't got none*, young master July',' he mocked, using a high-pitched voice to imitate the nun. 'And don't use the word — *ain't*! People will think you didn't have any schooling at all!' 'He grinned. 'I reckon I kind of slipped back to using the same language as T L does. You know how, if you're around someone long enough, you tend to pick up their style of talking.'

'Yes, I've noticed as much.'

He bobbed his head. 'As Sister Thelma is my witness, Miss Valeron, I know how to speak more proper. I've listened to a speech or two and read a few books over the years. I'll sure work on eliminating ain't and other bad grammar words from my talking. Is there anything else I do that digs a spur into your flanks?'

It was Wendy's turn to laugh. 'I wasn't aware I had flanks — though I've been called a filly a time or two.'

July's eyes sparkled. 'I'll bet it was always intended as a compliment.'

The door opened and Dutch stuck his head outside. 'We're clearing the table for Mildred,' he said simply. 'Figured you two might be finished by now.'

'By all means!' Wendy told him. 'July needs to get some sleep, after being on night watch.'

'Don't usually have a night rider,' Dutch admitted. 'But, after the rustlers hit — well, it's a precaution for the time being.'

'No explanation is necessary,' Wendy said, taking both her plate and the plate and cup from July. 'I'll help clear the table. Then I've got a mountain of record books to go over.'

'I'm beholden to you for the meal, Miss Valeron,' July said quickly. 'Be sure to tell the cook it's the best breakfast I ever et. Uh,' he corrected quickly, 'best meal I ever ate.'

Wendy smiled at him for the effort. 'I will, and good day to you, Mr Colby.'

Locke was standing near Reb's desk as Wendy entered the room. She had helped Dutch clear the table and was ready to start her second day's work.

'How is the bookkeeping going, my dear?' was his opening volley.

Wendy could tell by his stance and the stern, but loving devotion in his eyes — this was going to be a special father-daughter chat.

'Before you begin the lecture about man and woman and life, Daddy, you should remember that I'm no longer a child.'

He smiled at her taking him on without hesitation. She was the only one in the family — other than Wanetta — who never blinked or caved in to his dominance.

'When it comes to courting, you're a very young twenty-two, Wendy,' he countered. 'How many male suitors have you had — two? Three?' He shook his head.

'And were any of those serious?'

Rather than enter a debate, Wendy took her usual position — that of the aggressor. 'There's something about July that intrigues me, Daddy. He is so basic, so honest. There's no pretense about him. He's one of those rare what-you-see-is-what-you-get kind of men.'

'I'd say we have a lot of those on the ranch and in our fair town.'

'Yes, but I'm related to most of them.'

He laughed. 'I'm not going to discourage you, daughter. My intention is to remind you not to think of July as a homeless puppy. A hard luck story and little boy smile can be beguiling. But I want you to look deeper. Boyish charm can entice a girl, but it's the man inside who will determine her happiness. You want a man who will stand by you through thick and thin, will work every day to make your dreams come true. He will be the father of your children, and you want a man for that job, not a footloose, immature boy.' He sighed. 'I am only concerned with you finding the right man, the one who will make you happy all the days of your life.'

Wendy remained patient until he presented his case. Rather than engage in verbal disputation, she walked up to him, rose up on her toes and placed a gentle kiss on his cheek.

Locke could not hide his pleasure at her show of affection. He gruffly cleared his throat, in an effort to maintain a strict visage.

'You don't have to worry about me, Daddy,' Wendy whispered softly. 'I am your daughter, and a Valeron. I'll make the right choice.'

Her father chuckled. 'Wasted my breath, didn't I.'

It was a statement, so Wendy replied: 'It shows me you love me. I don't think that is ever wasting your breath.'

He didn't blush, as that would not have been masculine, but the facial gesture reminded her of a somewhat uncertain man, one who had encountered a puzzle and had no idea how the pieces fit together.

'I'll leave you to your work, daughter. If you should need me, I'll be staying close to the house today.'

'OK, Daddy,' she cooed. 'Thanks for sharing your sage advice.'

He presented a dour expression. 'And I'm sure you'll ignore every word.'

'Nonsense,' she countered. 'I'll give it the same amount of consideration as everything else you have ever told me.'

He waved a hand and turned about, but she caught a glimpse of the smile that came to his face.

4

It had begun to rain during the afternoon and continued until it grew dark. Being experienced and practical, Jared and Shane threw up a lean-to on the leeward side of a rocky butte. They were high enough up the side of the hill not to worry about a flash-flood, and they picketed their horses where they could eat the local vegetation. The rainfall continued throughout the night and into the next morning, so they took their time getting started. With little dry kindling, they consumed a cold meal of hard tack and beans, while waiting out the worst of the storm.

'The cattle were headed toward the river,' Jared outlined, after a time. 'I suspect them vermin crossed ahead of this storm. There's nothing west of here but mountains and a few small settlements.'

'The rustlers appear to be heading out of Colorado,' Shane suggested. 'What if they continue into Utah or New Mexico?'

'Fifty head of steers and committing murder,' Jared recounted their crimes. 'That's not the action of a would-be rancher. Can't start a herd with only steers, and they can't ship them back east with a known brand. That Double-B is next to impossible to alter.'

Shane frowned. 'You figure they are driving them to a meat-packing house of some kind?'

'I'll bet you a dime to your dollar they turn back towards Denver. Either there or Colorado Springs.'

'Do you know of any slaughterhouses in those areas?'

Jared shook his head. 'I didn't spend much time in Denver, other than when we were helping Trina get her life and ranch back. But you know they get their meat from somewhere. Denver has miners, farmers, ranchers and all manner of businesses. With the railroad going through, they are pretty much the major hub for a hundred miles around.'

Shane grinned. 'I've heard of the fancy parlors and the girls over on Market Street.'

'Yep, you'll find a lot of girls ready to fleece a man with money, and plenty of gambling joints to take anything he has left.'

'I never asked you before — you ever visited those types of places?'

Jared grinned. 'I've lost a few dollars at the gaming tables — that what you're talking about?'

Shane snickered. 'You know that's not it. The women. I'm talking about buying a gal's favors.'

Being six years older than Shane, Jared always considered his cousin like he would have a younger brother. He could have made up some stories — from things he had heard from others — but he didn't.

'I've bought a girl a drink or two and done a little dancing on occasion, Shane,' he said. 'But I never felt the urge to pay for a woman's favors. To me, holding a girl tight and kissing her — maybe doing a lot more — it don't mean a thing unless you have feelings for her.'

Shane chuckled. 'This from a guy who's the oldest bachelor in the family.'

'I wouldn't think less of you, if you wanted to visit one of those places,' he told his cousin. 'I'm just saying, it isn't for me.'

Shane stared out at the continual drizzle. 'Any man would be happy with a gal like Brett's wife — she's pretty as can be and has got a beautiful singing voice. Even so, I'd be satisfied with what Martin has — a good woman, as sweet and gentle as a lamb. Add two or three kids and who could ask for more?'

'I'd take either of those, or Trina too,' Jared agreed. 'Shucks, I'd be equally happy to find me a girl like Marie, Reese's wife.'

'I don't know . . . she belonged to an Indian,' Shane said hesitantly. 'I want to be . . . well, the first man to . . . ' He didn't finish the statement.

Jared laughed out loud but not to mock him. 'You have a right to expect that, Cuz. You're about as pure as the driven snow. I'll bet you've never even kissed a girl.'

'Have too!' Shane defended himself.

'Who?' Jared shot back. 'I've never heard of you actually courting a gal. Who could you have kissed?'

'Um, well,' Shane displayed his embarrassment. 'Maria,' he answered after a pause. 'We kissed a few times.'

Jared could have made light of that, as Maria had been courted by several of the ranch hands. She and Veta did laundry and housekeeping — they were both looking for a husband.

'Yeah, I remember when you and her were he-ing and she-ing. Maria would like to be a member of the Valeron family.'

Shane sighed. 'She came across as a little too eager. I got the feeling she wanted my last name more than she wanted me.'

'Trust me, Cuz,' Jared told him. 'When you find the right gal, she will plant a kiss on your lips that will make your knees weak.'

'Ah, you're joshing me,' Shane said. 'I can't see something as simple as a kiss doing that.'

'From the right gal, one you have a hankering for — it sure can. Like I said, I've been there before. It's something you don't soon forget.'

'So, how do you know when to. . . ?' he stumbled over the question. 'I mean, you've never had a steady girl, a favorite. Not that I know of anyway.'

'It was a long time back, when Reese and I were in Cheyenne. We had taken in a hundred head of steers to ship back east.' He allowed the memory to unfold, experiencing the feeling once more. 'We joined in at a party — some rancher Pa knew pretty well. The man had a daughter, but she was only sixteen.' He sighed. 'Well, the two of us did quite a bit of dancing, then sneaked out the back door for some fresh air.'

'And she up and kissed you?'

He shook his head. 'It wasn't like that. I mean, I knew she was too young to know her true feelings about a man.

Shucks, her father had been careful to keep her away from menfolk, wanting her to be fully grown before he allowed her to court. But the two of us . . . ' He heaved another sigh. 'Man o' mama! She really curled my socks.'

'How come you never went back for her?'

He shrugged. 'Time passed. And now? I've hanged or killed a number of men. Deserving or not, I don't feel worthy of a gal as innocent and virtuous as her. That's what I'm saying about Marie — I wouldn't be all that picky about my wife's history, not if she loves me.'

'Yeah, I see.' Shane grinned. 'You've got a temper too. I don't remember the last time I cussed anyone out.'

'I believe it was the day that one new-hire took a rope to swat at Beauty, 'cause he didn't like her tossing his hat!'

Shane chuckled. 'You're right. I was ready to light into him about that.' He shrugged. 'I should have warned him about the mare's playful antics.'

'You and that horse put on a good

show for the folks' anniversary. Won't ever hear me argue about how much memory a horse has. Beauty was just as good as the time you had her perform at Brimstone.'

'Wonderful animal,' Shane praised. 'It's a shame she's getting along in years. I'll bet I could make a lot of money traveling around and doing a show with her.'

'Well, enough of this pining and day-dreaming.' Jared turned to the business at hand. 'Let's get our slickers on. We need to keep on the trail of those cattle.'

'The rain has already washed away most of the tracks. What if this storm destroys what little tracks we have to follow?' Shane uttered a groan. 'Besides which, if the rustlers have already crossed the river it's gonna be too high for us to ford with all of this rain.'

'Animals always leave a trail,' Jared replied confidently. 'It might be a track or two under the shelter of a sagebrush, or a cow patty that doesn't quite wash away. No, sir. We'll follow them until they reach their destination — no matter how long it takes!'

* * *

Singeon Pegg counted out the remainder of the money he had promised Mantee. The man stuck the wad of bills into his jacket and showed a wide grin.

'This is gonna keep us in high style for a few weeks. How long before you can use another fifty head?'

'If you grab that many again, you'll have to keep them at the ranch to graze for a spell. It will be at least a month before I can move so much meat and catch up with the rendering from the last bunch. It takes time to process so many head at one time. And I told you, if I end up shipping product to another city, I end up working for nothing.'

'Too bad,' Mantee said. 'That Barrett ranch had at least fifty more steers ready to send to market. With a couple of the boys knowing the ins and outs of the place, we could hit them a second time and pick up the rest of the herd.'

Pegg's brow wrinkled in thought. 'Barrett?' he repeated the name. 'That's where these beef came from?'

'Yeah. You remember — used to be run by a snotty-nosed kid, Robby Gowan, and his mother. They didn't know which way was up when it came to ranching.' He guffawed. 'Boy-howdy, that there Robbie and a couple of men used to round up a few head and sell them real cheap. I used to buy ten or twenty head on the sly for less than half of what they were worth, just 'cause he wanted some spending money. Rex and Dekay earned more working for him than the ranch work paid them.' He shrugged. 'When the Barrett gal got her place back, Rex and Dekay were fired. They joined up with us right after that.'

'Barrett you say?' Pegg scowled in thought. 'I remember reading something about the Barrett situation in the Denver paper.' A sudden chill rushed up his spine. 'That was Trina Barrett's place — the gal Robbie and his mother tried to have stuck in that crooked lunatic asylum!'

Mantee grunted. 'Yep, that's the one.'

Pegg's eyes bugged. He unexpectedly leapt forward and grabbed two fistfuls of Mantee's jacket front. 'Are you out of your mind!' he wailed, shaking him violently. 'Holy hell, Mantee! Do you know what you've done?'

The rustler stumbled backward from the sudden assault. 'What?' he cried. 'What!'

'Trina Barrett married a Valeron a couple months back. One of *the* Valerons!'

Mantee's complexion blanched. 'The Valerons,' he muttered their name almost reverently. 'Ah, for the love of . . .' He slowly shook his head back and forth. 'I didn't know, Pegg! I didn't know!'

Pegg placed a hand on his forehead, trembling with a sudden and uncontrollable panic. 'We've got to work fast,' he rasped. 'This is bad! Very bad!'

'Rex and Dekay didn't say nothing about the gal hitching her wagon to . . .'

Pegg waved the man to silence. 'It's too late for laying blame — we've got to act!'

Mantee showed a cowed expression. 'Tell me what you need us to do.'

'You get your boys over here and lend Everett a hand — we need every one of those beef gone — and I mean right now!' Mantee bobbed his head eagerly and Pegg continued. 'Soon as the last steer is skinned, you gather up every last hide and get them all over to the tannery. Tell Hank to process them immediately. We can't allow a single one of those hides to be seen while the brand is readable. You tell him our lives — and his! — depend on it.'

'We'll get it done!' Mantee promised, licking his lips in trepidation. 'Me and the boys will do exactly as you say.'

'Let's hope we have enough time.'

Mantee bobbed his head a second time. 'We made a trail halfway to the Western Slope before we crossed the river and come back. Figure at the least, a four- or five-day head start. It means we should be in the clear for at least another two or three days — that's even if some tracking fool does manage to follow those beef.'

'Get after it!' Pegg reiterated. 'And make damn sure Hank understands the importance of getting those hides processed!'

Mantee rotated to go out the office door, but Pegg stopped him. 'And one more thing,' he warned. 'Soon as those cattle are taken care of, you best pick up a few head of stock, enough to make it look like you have some cattle on hand. If the Valerons start snooping around, you will want to look legitimate.'

'I hear you,' he replied. 'We'll buy a few head and stick our brand on them.'

Pegg watched the man leave and began to pace the floor. He would have to ask his father to help, along with the Gallegos woman, and work with Larson himself. That was an awful lot of beef to process, and they had very little time to get the job done. He slammed his fist into an open palm.

Of all the fouled-up messes — the Valerons! He stopped long enough to stare at the closed door. Another worry. Mantee said they had killed a couple of cowpunchers when they stole the small herd. If it was only stolen cattle, there was a chance the Valerons would give up the hunt . . . in time. But if Mantee and his boys had killed someone close to the Valerons?

Pegg swore under his breath. He knew, if that were the case, they would never quit. Eventually, him, Mantee, and even Hank Grubber would pay the full price. From everything he'd read or heard about the Valerons, when one of their own was harmed, they didn't quit until they had extracted full and total retribution.

* * *

Don dragged himself through the door, so tired he had nearly fallen asleep on the ride home. It was all he could do to put his horse in the small corral and make sure there was plenty of grain and water. He wasn't surprised to find Gayle had been dozing on their worn divan. She jumped up at his entering the house and hurried over to put her arms around him.

'Donny!' she murmured. 'I thought you'd never get home!'

'It's been a very tough week,' he said. 'I never cut and packaged so much beef in my life.' He hugged her briefly, then moved to the kitchen and collapsed on to a chair.

'I've got some fresh bread and leftover stew warming on the stove,' his wife told him. 'I didn't know when you would get home.'

He heaved a heavy sigh. 'I'll try and eat a few bites . . . if I can stay awake.'

'What is going on?' his wife lamented, stepping back to study his haggard condition. 'You go to work at daylight and don't get home until ten or eleven at night. You can't keep this up!'

'It'll be easier in a few more days,' he told her, taking a chair at the table. 'The locker is the fullest I've ever seen — must be sixty sides of beef hanging in there. I didn't know it would hold that many.'

Gayle began to dish up a generous portion of stew onto Don's waiting plate. 'But working on Sunday? Mr Pegg can't expect you to work these horrific hours for much longer. You'll be down sick from lack of rest and sleep!'

Don took a bite and began to chew. 'Like I said, it's real strange. Both Pegg and his father, along with Mrs Gallegos, worked with me to cut and package the meat most of the day again. We don't even have orders for most of the stuff. Three extra guys lent Everett a hand, plus his usual helper. Ingram has both of his cousins working for him and Louie hauled a ton of meat into town to try and get rid of it at a discount price. That's not the way Pegg operates.' He grunted. 'He only cuts his prices to run somebody out of business — like he did us!'

'I haven't heard of any new meat markets opening,' Gayle said.

'No . . . this is something else. Everett

mentioned that Pegg told him he wanted to get rid of the beef in the holding corral as fast as he could. When I asked him if he knew why, he said there must have been a special demand from the tannery. He finished off the last of the cattle today, and one of the men who usually works at the Big M ranch left with a wagon full of hides for Hank's tannery, and it was already dark. I mean, this makes no sense at all.'

'Maybe Everett is right. There might be a huge order for hides and the tannery needed to fill it in a hurry.' His wife remained thoughtful. 'Or it could be the need for tallow.'

Don sighed. 'I don't know. Tallow demand is a possibility, but it takes quite a long time to cure the hides, what with the soaking, removing the hair, and the rest of the process. I have to wonder how many hides they can handle at one time.'

'Are you going to get paid extra for working Sunday?'

'Pegg promised both Everett and me two or three days off this coming week and a little bonus as compensation for the extra hours. I don't know about Ingram.' Don managed a weary grin. 'Maybe you can get the kids the new shoes you've been wanting to buy.'

'They can do without new shoes,' she grumbled, 'so long as they have a father! I hate seeing you work this hard.'

'Like I said, honey,' he soothed her ire, 'the worst is about over. With the balance of the meat in the locker, we should be back to simply filling the weekly orders in a day or two.'

Gayle offered him her usual supporting smile. 'I'll be looking forward to those days off. We might even work in a picnic or fishing trip with the kids.'

'Sounds great!'

'Now you finish up and get off to bed. You're only going to get five or six hours sleep . . . and I don't want you too tired to enjoy the time off!'

Don finished the last bite from his plate, kissed his wife, then headed for bed. His back ached from bending over the chopping table, his hands were so stiff he couldn't make a fist, from using the cutting knives and doing packaging, and even his legs complained from the long hours of standing.

He collapsed on to the bed, thinking he would be asleep by the time his head hit the pillow. But the nagging concerns remained. What did it mean, all the drive and haste concerning this last batch of cattle? Something surely wasn't right.

5

The two Valeron men left their horses and crept forward on foot. After studying the place for a short time, Jared grunted his disappointment.

'We missed our chance. The cattle were only at the ranch west of here overnight — no more than a day or two, before they ended up here.'

'The pasture next to that old ranch house still had grass and all of the cow chips were fresh,' Shane agreed. 'It's for certain the steers weren't kept there very long.'

'It's the end of the trail.' Jared remarked, pointing to the empty holding corral behind two buildings. 'That's where the Double B cattle met their end.'

'Looks like a fair-sized slaughterhouse,' Shane said. 'What about that blocky building on one side? It looks like it's made out of railroad ties.'

'Storage house of some kind — probably a meat locker.'

'I've heard of them, but never seen one. Must be like the new railroad cars, the ones that keep meat and fruit cold.'

Jared sighed. 'Dag-nabit! Not a single steer left.' He studied the place a bit longer. 'And the freight wagon bed is empty — not a hide in sight either.'

'Already shipped to a tanning place?' Shane wondered. 'They must have worked awfully fast. We couldn't be more than three or four days behind them.'

'Yes, it hurt us, having to wait a half-day for the water to drop enough to cross the river. The cattle thieves got across before the heavy rain.'

'So what now?' Shane wanted to know. 'Do we go in there tomorrow with guns drawn and demand answers?'

'Tip our hand and we lose what little surprise we have on our side. From the looks of it, this slaughterhouse has been here a long time. That means the owner likely has contacts and support in Denver.'

'Pa told us how the city was wide open for a good many years,' Shane recalled the stories. 'Big business, gambling halls, a few crime bosses running things . . . even after the police department was formed.'

'In a city of any size, there's always a few corrupt men in positions of power. However, Pa knows Governor Pitkin. That will give us some leverage of our own.'

'To do what?'

'Brands have to be registered,' Jared pointed out. 'That means we not only have a bunch of murdering rustlers, it would appear we also have a crooked slaughterhouse and maybe a tannery to deal with as well. Can't go after one without the other.'

'It's a big place!' Shane declared. 'The corral would easily hold fifty head of cattle!'

'The tannery is probably a good-sized operation too.'

'Jer, these people probably do business with every store, shop, market, hotel, work-gang and mining company for miles around!'

'Yes, they provide a lot of meat, but that doesn't mean they don't have competition. Plus, with the governor on our side, the law will have to do their job — whether they are inclined to look the other way or not.'

'OK, cuz,' Shane said. 'You've obviously got some kind of plan. I'll follow your lead.'

'Soon as someone figures out that we're involved, they are going to be watching the ranch and keeping an eye peeled for any of us Valerons.'

A light glimmered in Shane's eyes. 'Hence the reason for all the hurry to get rid of the beef and hides.'

'That would be my guess,' Jared said. 'I believe it's best to play this like a game of tag in the dark — if they don't see or hear you move, the guy who's watching for you won't know where you are.'

'Speaking of dark, we wouldn't have seen this place if not for the lights. It looks as if someone is still there.'

'Likely a night watchman. They probably have a full meat locker.'

'There were a couple guys leaving when we first arrived. How long do we wait? It's plain to see they're finished with all of the killing and skinning.'

'And the hides are already gone.' Jared rubbed his stubble of beard, the remnant of having not shaved for several days.

'What now?' Shane wanted to know.

'Let's find the tannery. If this is their main supplier, it will likely be a couple miles down the road.'

It took thirty minutes and was well past midnight by the time Jared and Shane approached the cluster of buildings. 'That's it,' Jared said quietly. 'You can tell by the smell — it's the tannery.'

'What now?'

'Let's tie off our horses over in that chaparral,' Jared directed, tipping his head at a secluded cove where the animals wouldn't be seen.'

Then we will have us a look-see.'

After a thorough check, they discovered there was a lone night watchman. He had retired to the office and was having coffee. They watched him for a few minutes, until he put his feet up on a desk and began reading the paper. After making a circle to stay out of his sight,

Jared and Shane reached the perimeter fence.

'Not the best of help,' Shane whispered. 'Someone could steal the stove out of the same room. He wouldn't notice till he got cold.'

'What's to watch?' Jared said. 'Probably hired to keep the wild animals away from the hides. There isn't much else of value to steal.'

'The five-foot fence around the perimeter would keep most larger animals out,' Shane replied. 'What are we looking for?'

Jared didn't reply to his question, climbing carefully over the fence. Once his cousin had done the same, he pointed to the beamhouse portion of the structures. 'Let's hope they have some hides that aren't already soaking in the liming solution. Once the hair and excess meat is removed, it will be next to impossible to prove where the hides came from.'

'Right! If we find some Double B brands. . .!'

The declaration didn't need completion. The phantom duo crossed the darkest part of the yard and found their way through an open window. The smell was enough it about gagged them. Both pulled their bandannas up over their noses to help fight the stench.

With a lighted match, they went through the building and checked the vats and stacks of hides. It appeared all of the hides had been either cleaned and de-haired or were soaking in the brine solution. Trying to determine the brand was a waste of time. Even so, Jared was certain these were Barrett cattle hides.

'Now what?' Shane asked, trying not in inhale. 'I don't see any fresh hides waiting to go into a vat. They've covered their tracks.'

Jared led the way back outside. It took but a glance to see the watchman was still reading the newspaper. They returned to their waiting horses the way they had come.

'Well, that was a bust,' Shane griped. 'You can bet they hurried the process as much as they could so there wouldn't be any evidence.'

'It's why we had to check it out tonight, rather than make the trip out to the ranch. I had hoped we could get a few branded hides as proof against the tannery and slaughterhouse. I'm guessing someone realized where these cattle came from. If they know we Valerons are involved, they will destroy all of the evidence as quickly as possible.'

'How could they know we are on their trail?'

'They might not,' Jared answered. 'If they didn't know the Double B was tied to our ranch, then this could have been a hurried job due to the fact the Barrett spread is not more than twenty-five to thirty miles away. Pretty brassy of them to peddle rustled cattle so close to the victim's ranch.'

'What's our next move?'

'I need to send a telegraph message to Pa. I have an idea that Wendy can lend us a hand with.'

'Wendy? You afraid someone will recognize you?' Shane asked.

'Wyatt and I made quite an impression

on the townspeople when we brought in those outlaws. There was even a photograph of us in the newspaper.'

'Right. It means we will have to be careful with our questioning too. Them at the slaughterhouse or tannery won't want to talk to us at all.'

'That's where Wendy comes in. You and me are going to speak to some of the local markets, although we'll try not to arouse any suspicion. I'd guess our best approach will be to pretend to be looking for the most inexpensive place to buy beef — claim we have a work gang laying some narrow-gauge tracks.'

'To do what?'

'Mining,' Jared replied. 'The narrow-gauge cars can go right into the mines, then deliver the ore to the railroad.'

'Maybe we ought to get Faro,' Shane mentioned their cousin. 'He's in charge of our family's mining.'

'No store owner is going to want to know the details. Their interest is in selling their merchandise. Besides, we are looking for a good deal, not just someone to provide the beef.'

'I see what you're saying,' Shane told him. 'What about your sister? How do we contact Wendy when she arrives?'

'We'll meet at the hotel. She will know to check in at the same one as we stayed at last time.'

'Then you and me are going to head into town and get a room for the night?'

Jared shrugged. 'Not if you'd prefer the fresh air and open sky over your head.'

'After being rained on, treading through an ocean of mud, crossing a river, then sleeping on a pile of rocks last night — I'll take a room. I don't care if it's a closet and a single blanket!'

'Hot dang! You're getting to be as soft as a daisy. Good thing you spend most of your time on the ranch.'

'Yeah, tell me about it, Jer. Tell me how you want to save a few dollars by sleeping in some hollow, then using creek water to wash and shave. And let's not forget we're down to a couple of tins of beans for breakfast.'

'Like I said, Shane. We deserve to spoil ourselves a little. Let's head for town.'

* * *

Locke entered the main sitting room, where Wendy was seated at a large desk in the corner. Reb had kept the records up to date, so she had been able to manage the books with little effort. She looked up at his entrance.

'Hi, Dad!' she said, thinking how much younger he looked. Taking charge of a small ranch was much easier on him than running the massive Valeron empire. Even the gray above his ears was less noticeable. 'Any word on Dodge today?'

'Just what Reb told us yesterday in his telegraph message. It sounded quite optimistic.'

She laughed. 'There's a word I never heard you say before.'

'Yes, well, you and Jared still live at home,' he reparteed. 'And with Cliff and the little muffin always around too, I sometimes lack optimism.'

He left the words hanging, so Wendy said: 'I for one am always optimistic.'

'Yes, you don't think there isn't anything you can't do. Jared gives me the same headache.'

'If Dodge gets back on his feet, he'll probably be returning to the ranch soon,' she opined. 'I imagine that will end our part of this adventure.'

Locke noticed the words were spoken with a hint of disappointment on his daughter's face. He deduced she didn't wish to pack up and return home, and that regret could be summed up in a single name — July Colby!

'Is that a telegraph message you're carrying?'

Locke nodded. 'Max ran over to the way station this morning to pick up the mail. He just got back.'

'But nothing from Reb?'

'No, but there is something else,' he informed Wendy. He pulled around an extra chair and sat down across from her. 'The wire is from Jared.'

'Did he locate the rustlers?' she asked eagerly.

'It's what the telegraph message is about,' he replied. Then he paused to study his daughter. She was a very similar image to his wife, Wanetta, at the same age. Same dazzling sparkle in the depths of her eyes, same petite sculpturing of her features, even the kindred enchanting lips and mouth. He loved Scarlet dearly, who was a little prettier than Wendy, but Scarlet had always been a proper lady — although strong in spirit and will. Wendy, contrarily, was like a forest nymph, darting this way and that, going here and there. She had wit and a knack for finding trouble — similar to her favorite brother, Jared. She deserved so much more than a wandering down-on-his-luck orphan cowhand.

'You were saying? About the telegram?' Wendy prompted him, curious when he didn't continue.

He almost laughed. That was so like her. Scarlet would have sat patiently and let him take his time. But Wendy — she always had things to do — in and out, busy, busy, busy. He idly wondered if any man would ever be able to keep up with her.

'Jared has asked for you to join him in Denver. He has a job for you.'

It was rare to see Wendy struck speechless, even for a moment. Locke could not even remember such a time.

'Uh,' Wendy's recovery was swift, her nimble mind already working on a thousand avenues at one time. 'Jer must have a special kind of problem if he's asking for me.'

'He didn't put too much into the cable, in case the telegrapher happened to be friends with the wrong sort of people.' Locke removed the message from his pocket and looked at it. 'The message reads: *Regards from Denver to Wendy and July . . . Stop. Inform Freddy of party . . . Stop. Will see cousins soon . . . Stop.* And it's signed Jared.'

Wendy shook her head in utter bewilderment. 'Regards to me and Mr Colby? Party? What on earth is he up to?'

Locke rubbed his chin thoughtfully. 'It's pretty straightforward, when you consider he couldn't be sure who might see the wire.'

She frowned. 'You and I have a completely different idea as to the meaning of *straightforward*!'

'Jared wants you and July to join him in Denver.'

Wendy skewed her expression and uttered an uncertain, 'Uh, OK.'

Locke continued. '*Freddy* obviously means Governor Frederick Pitkin. I'm to contact him and have him support whatever scheme Jared has come up with.'

'Well, of course,' Wendy said, sarcastically. 'Everyone calls the Governor of the State of Colorado by his childhood nickname!'

'And the part about the *cousins* means he wants me to have some help ready at hand.'

'All right, so the men in this family all talk in some kind of code. I get that. But what about me and July? What could he possibly want with our new hired man?'

'My guess,' Locke mused, 'he needs someone who is not connected with either our ranch or the Barrett ranch.'

Wendy gave an unladylike snort. 'Now I know why you and Jerry should never be partners when we're playing Pinochle! I'll bet you both know what cards the other is holding before the bids even start!'

'My dear, you don't think your brother and I would stoop to — as you put it — use some sort of secret code to win at a game of cards.'

'I darn well do!'

Locke cast aside the banter. 'I sent Max back to telegraph Reb. He needs to come to the ranch tonight. Dutch is going to inform young Mr Colby to also join us when he comes in from the range. We'll get this thing organized.'

'Where did Jerry send the message from?'

'Denver, of course.'

She frowned. 'He's twenty miles away and sends us a telegraph message instead of coming to the ranch?'

'I suspect he will explain his reasons when he sees you.'

'But why me and July? What can we do that he can't?'

'Your brother must have a plan, Wendy.' Then, with a touch of the Valeron wit: 'Without sitting across from him at the card table, I can hardly be expected to know what is in his mind.'

She shook her head, mystified. 'It's only a four-hour ride. It makes no sense to contact us by telegraph.'

'Like I said, you can ask him when you see him.'

'I darn well will!'

* * *

Pegg arrived home to find his mother had a stew warming on the stove. No matter how she felt, the woman refused to be waited on, or allow anyone else to do what she considered to be her job.

'Mom, you didn't have to fix my supper. I've told you before, I can always get by with some bread and fruit or whatever.'

'You and Bing have worked so very hard lately,' she argued. 'I mean, you let him come home at a decent hour, then sometimes you don't come home at all.'

'I've got an old couch in the storage room. When it gets too late, I simply don't make the trip.' Pegg shrugged. 'And I always keep some food around. After all, we process meat for a living.'

'Oh, I'm sure you can use the pot-bellied stove in the office to fry up a piece of raw meat. What a fine meal that is!'

He didn't reply, but walked over and gave his mother a hug. 'How you feeling today?'

'It helps when the nights are cooler. I swear, I sometimes think women who die young are doing it out of cowardice. It's like constantly running a fever, and the headaches and other ailments . . .' She sighed. 'Good thing I have your father. I'd hate to go through something like this on my own.'

'Pa in bed already?'

'You worked him until he about fell

asleep at the dinner table. He's not as young as he used to be.'

'I'm beat too,' Pegg admitted. 'But we got the job done and, hopefully, we won't have a rush order like that again.'

'Sit down and I'll dish you up some stew. I made some of you favorite cookies for dessert.'

'You're too good to me, Mom.'

'Better wash your hands,' she ordered. 'I don't want you thinking those cookies smell like dried blood or something.'

'I wish you would let me have Miss Devonshire come in more than once a week to do laundry. She could help with the housework or cooking. It's got to be hard on you, when you're feeling poorly.'

'Don't you worry about me, Singeon.' Then with a twinkle in her eye, 'If you want to get me someone to share the work, find yourself a wife. Bing and I wouldn't mind becoming grandparents.'

He laughed, as if her suggestion was a joke, and wandered over to the washbasin. He knew she was serious, but Pegg was no prize. Quite overweight, with a receding hairline — thanks to his grandparents on Lajetta's side — and he was forced to wear spectacles when reading or doing paperwork. He also looked part bulldog, with a wide, flat nose, sagging jowls, and had more facial hair than most women cared for. When you consider he was dogmatic and short-tempered — only a woman who wanted his money would take him for a husband.

The idea struck him as funny. When he had enough money to buy a wife, he would rather spend it on a dozen different parlor girls. At least them he could pay and be done with.

* * *

Squint and Rocco entered the small ranch house. Pierce Mantee was still up, smoking a cigar and sitting in a creaky rocking chair, with a pillow to support his back. While only in his thirties, a life on the move, so many hours in the saddle or sleeping on the cold, damp ground aged a man quick and caused numerous aches and pains.

Squint was the one to speak. 'Watching the slaughterhouse paid off. A pair of shadows showed up last night sniffing around. They sure 'nuff tracked them beef all the way to Pegg's. Reckon they seen they was too late, 'cause they next headed over to the tannery.'

Rocco bobbed his head. 'Can't be no doubt. They looked to have been on the trail at least a week or so. They didn't spend no time at Pegg's, but they were more thorough at the tannery. We seen them sneak in for a look around, but they only stayed for a few minutes.'

'Trying to find evidence of the Double B beef,' Mantee surmised. 'Did they come out with any hides?'

'Not a thing,' Rocco assured him. 'Hank did like he was told — didn't leave nothing lying about to tie him to those cattle.'

'Where are the two men now?'

Squint answered: 'They went into town and got a room at the Dead-End hotel. We took turns keeping watch the rest of the night, but they never left. Come daylight we headed back here to report in.'

'They could go to the law?' Rocco suggested.

'Pegg has a man who will let him know if anything comes up,' Mantee vowed with confidence. 'He pays a handsome sum each month to keep any badges from snooping around his operation.'

'You want we should arrange an accident for them two trackers?'

'Not yet. Pegg worked his men long hours to see there was no trail to follow. And like you said, Hank Grubber is good at his job over at the tannery too. You can bet there will be no trail to follow.'

'What do you want us to do?' Rocco asked.

'Rex and Dekay worked at the Barrett ranch. Have them keep an eye on the two bloodhounds and see if they recognize them. I'd like to know who is doing the tracking . . . just in case we have to deal with them.'

'I'll ride with them to Denver and point out the two trackers for the boys,' Rocco said. 'I got better eyesight than Squint.'

'What fer do you think I squints for?' the man complained. 'I kin see close-up, just not off in the distance.'

'Rocco, you handle it, but tell Dekay and Rex not to be seen.' Mantee leaned forward in his chair and frowned. 'We want to be darn certain we don't draw any suspicion on us.'

'You think one of them might be a Valeron?' Squint asked, his voice little more than a whisper, as if he was afraid the name would make one of them appear in the flesh.

'That's why I want Rex and Dekay to have a look at them. Both of them claimed to have seen a couple of the Valerons when the ranch changed hands.'

'We maybe ought to skedaddle from these parts,' Squint said. 'I don't much favor the idea of butting heads with the Valerons.'

'The Dead-End hotel is the cheapest place to stay in Denver,' Rocco said.

'With the money that family has, I can't see them staying there instead of one of the better places.'

'Might be trying to stay concealed, keep anyone from knowing they are around,' Mantee surmised.

'Damn,' Rocco sighed. 'Who could have known the Valerons would be part of this? Rex said the Barrett gal got the ranch back after her stepmother and Robby were out of the picture. He and Dekay were both fired for having helped the son sell cattle on the side. We had no way of knowing the Valerons still had an interest in the Barrett ranch.'

'It's a little late to worry about that end of things now,' Mantee said. 'One thing's certain, we're not going after any more of their cattle. And I don't care what those two meatheads have to say about it!'

6

It was after dinner when everyone gathered for the meeting. July, Wendy, Locke and Reb were seated round the family room. Reb was in a good mood, as Dodge had sat up and shared a meal with him. The outlook was good and the doctor recommended only another couple days before he could start exercising and take short walks. If everything went to schedule, he would be going home in two weeks or less.

'About the rustlers,' Reb spoke, after everyone was settled. 'Dodge and me have done some serious contemplation.' He squinted about at the others, but spoke to Locke. 'And we done reached a conclusion, boss.'

'I'm not your boss at this ranch,' Locke told him.

Reb grinned. 'Mr Valeron, long as I live, you'll always be the Boss to me.'

Locke chuckled. 'What were you saying about a conclusion?'

'When we took over this here ranch, Miss Barrett had Max and a decent cowhand or two. There were also a couple jokers who had supported and worked with that conniving old witch and her misbegotten son. We up and fired them both 'cause we didn't trust them no more'n a bee-stung mule. Rex and Dekay were sorry excuses for ranch hands, and Max told Dodge he reckoned they had been in on every shady deal Rob and his mother were mixed up in.'

'Is this leading someplace?' Locke encouraged him to get to the point.

'We got a notion them two might be mixed up in this rustling,' Reb explained. 'They knew when we would gather the steers for roundup, when they were to be sold, and where the holding pasture was. Add to that, they done shot Dodge and young Lonnie. They could have jumped them and tied them up or something, but they started shooting, intending to kill them right off.'

'Because Dodge would have recognized them,' Locke reasoned.

'That's our thinking.'

'Which is all the more reason Jared and Shane have to stay in the shadows,' Wendy suggested. 'Those men could be watching for them.'

'I can only guess why Jared would send a wire when he could have ridden here in a matter of hours,' Locke determined. 'But he could be acting on that very assumption — someone might be watching.'

'So why include me?' July asked. 'I mean, your boy didn't say ten words to me on the way here. Any idea what my part is supposed to be in this?'

Locke grunted his ignorance, but Reb raised a hand like a child in a school classroom. It brought a frown from Locke.

'Reb,' he said sternly, 'we are guests in your house! You don't have to ask permission to speak.'

'I've an idea as to what your boy's plan might be — the first part anyway.' At Locke's approving nod, he went on. 'As for the young feller here — he isn't known around town.' Turning his attention to Wendy, 'You remember, we all stayed at that big hotel across from the bank. I'm guessing Jared is figuring to meet you on the sly. If he's not staying at that hotel, he'll certainly expect you to get a room there.'

'I believe you're right on both counts, Reb,' Wendy said. 'We'll check in to the hotel and wait for Jerry to contact us.'

July showed a sheepish expression. 'I hope we aren't supposed to go as . . . you know, a married couple.'

'Jerry wouldn't do that!' Wendy stated emphatically.

Locke barked his own sentiment. 'No, he darn well wouldn't!'

'I'm sure he has something else in mind.' Wendy displayed a pixie simper, dissolving her father's glare. 'And you can bet it has to do with your contacting the governor.'

Locke, as always, was completely disarmed by his daughter's charm. 'I'll write a letter first thing in the morning. Wendy, you can see he gets it personally.'

'Youngster,' Reb asked July bluntly, 'can you shoot?'

'I've done a little hunting and the like — but nothing to brag about.'

'I'm a good shot,' Wendy piped up.

Locke snorted. 'Jared isn't going to put you two in a position where you have to fight. He asked for help, so I sent off a couple wires. If Wyatt isn't available, Troy and Faro can lend a hand. Dodge was like family, and every one of the single men on the ranch will come to Denver if need be.'

'You can count me in too,' Reb volunteered. 'I've a score to settle with them murdering scoundrels!'

Locke waited, but no one else spoke up. He stretched, weary from another long day and announced: 'It's time for bed. Does anyone have anything else to add?' purposely looking at July. 'You have any other questions, Colby?'

'No, sir! I'm proud to help in any way I can.'

'All right then, let's call it a night.'

* * *

Jared and Shane had taken an old one-time rooming house near the railroad station. Jared thought it better not to be sharing the same hotel as Wendy. It was going to be risky enough simply to visit the place and make contact with her and July. Perhaps it was only nerves, but Jared had been feeling a prickling sensation up the back of his neck as if they were being watched. He explained it to Shane, as their second day in Denver had passed uneventfully.

'Who could it be?' Shane asked, when he had finished.

'This outfit might have been rustling cattle for some time. Who knows how long the slaughterhouse has been dealing stolen beef? We have to assume they watch everyone coming to town by way of the southern or western route.'

'And you let me think we were saving Pa a few bucks by staying in that old, rat-infested lodging, instead of the plush hotel where you stayed with Wendy and

Reb.'

He shrugged. 'I didn't want you worrying about it. As I told you, I haven't actually seen anyone trailing after us. It's a feeling, nothing more.'

'Wendy ought to arrive today sometime,' Shane said. 'How we gonna contact her without being seen?'

'As we were wandering the streets, I took notice of a few options. We should be able to lose anyone trying to keep an eye on us. Once we have our meeting with her, we will trick anyone watching us into giving themselves away.'

'How's that?'

'I was thinking we would get our horses and take a ride out into open country.'

'What good would that do, Jer?'

'Put yourself in the place of whoever is keeping an eye on us. We wander around town a bit, suddenly disappear, then show up again. Only instead of going to our rooms, we light out as if we have found something out. We make a point of hurrying as much as we can.'

'OK — with you so far.'

'What would you do, Cuz?' Jared wanted to know. 'If you were charged with keeping track of us and we suddenly grabbed our horses and took off?'

Shane turned the scenario over in his head. 'Guess I'd either report back to my boss, or I'd follow after you to learn what you were up to.'

'Exactly.'

'Oh, I get it,' Shane said. 'They follow — we grab them.'

'Grab 'em or follow them to their boss. Depends on what or who shows up and what they do.'

'And if no one shows up?'

'We return to the stable and head for the sack.' He clicked his tongue. 'Remember, I haven't actually seen anyone. But it could be two or three guys taking turns. That makes it harder to know if you're being watched or not.'

'All right, how do we get to the fancy, comfortable, the I-wish-we-were-staying-there hotel without being followed?'

Jared explained. 'The saloon on Market Street has two entrances, one facing the main street and one facing the street behind it. We go in one door and out the other. A couple streets further down, there is a casino with two main exits. We do the same thing again.'

'If they are watching from two sides on the first one . . . ' Shane began.

'We'll lose them on the second,' Jared finished.

'I'm with you. Let's start the rock rolling down the hill and see how many quail we can flush.'

* * *

July stood with the curtain pulled to the side just enough to peek out. He had been in such a position since he entered Wendy's room.

'I wish I'd have gotten a room that overlooked the main street too,' he said to Wendy.

'If I know my brother, you probably wouldn't see him anyway.' She sighed. 'You might as well sit down. Jer will be knocking at the door any minute.'

July cocked his head and looked over his shoulder. 'All the more reason I ought to be standing here by the window.'

Wendy laughed. 'You're not afraid of my brother, are you?'

'You might as well ask me if I'm afraid of getting wet when caught in a down-pour of rain. Jared being around causes me genuine concern about minding my manners and keeping my distance around you.'

'And if it was just you and me?' she baited him. 'Are you saying you would behave differently?'

July chuckled. 'If you mean, were you not a Valeron, but maybe a waitress or maid?'

'Are you in the habit of chasing hotel maids?'

His grin widened. 'Never stayed in a hotel before, Miss Valeron, and that's the truth.'

Wendy narrowed her look. 'Hum . . . that's an evasion.'

'A what?'

'You are avoiding the question, not

denying that you would chase after maids or servants.'

'Let's say I have done a little chasing of female sorts, but never one as pretty and smart as you.'

'You think I'm smart?'

'Your Pa and Jared must,' he replied. 'They sent you here with me as your escort. I'm supposed to sit in the game, but you are the one they trust to play the cards.'

'Being educated isn't the same as being smart,' she explained her philosophy to July. 'Dodge never learned to read or write, but he's the smartest man around cattle that you will ever meet. My father could barely scribble his own name when he and his two brothers started up our ranch. Now he oversees an empire, with logging, mining, farming and ranching — not to mention a dozen businesses in Valeron. If you were to ask him if he was smart, he'd tell you he is as dumb as an ear of corn.'

'I see your point, Miss Valeron. Being smart on a subject or two don't make a person the brightest candle in a room.'

'And, if Jerry didn't think you could do whatever he has in mind, he would not have asked for you.' She gestured confidently. 'Which means he thinks you are smart enough to handle it.'

July grinned. 'I'm beginning to hope he needs someone who knows the quickest way to get his boot into his mouth. I reckon I could do that much without trying.'

Wendy laughed. She might have said something about his wit, but a light tap came at the door. It was time to get serious.

July put his hand on his gun and hurried over to stand next to the entrance. 'State your business,' he said, loud enough it would be heard on the other side of the door.

The words, 'Open up or kiss your teeth goodbye!' came from Jared's muffled voice on the other side.

July quickly pulled back the deadbolt and allowed Shane and Jared to enter. Both were grinning.

'Finding a strange man in my sister's hotel room could cause us kinfolk dire concern,' Jared stated firmly, though humor still shone in his eyes.

Wendy didn't force July to squirm under the pretended inquisition. She hurried over from the bed and gave Jared a hug of greeting. Then stepping back, she used a firm tone of voice. 'We were beginning to think you were lying in a ditch somewhere. It's nearly dark.'

'We had to wait until there were enough customers in the saloons to lose a shadow.'

Alarm entered her expression. 'Someone is following you?'

Jared told her of his suspicions. 'We've yet to see anyone, but we will check it out when we leave here.'

'What about us?' Wendy asked. 'Why are we here?'

'Did you get hold of the governor?'

She frowned. 'Father deciphered your absurd word-puzzle telegram. I'll never play against the two of you at cards again.'

He grinned. 'Did you get the message —'

She held up her hand to stop him. 'Contacted his office this morning,' she informed him. 'Father still has a lot of pull. An aide showed up early this afternoon with this.'

Opening her handbag, she dug out an important-looking piece of paper. It had the letterhead for the Governor's office and was signed by Pitkin himself.

Jared read it over and gave a nod of approval. 'OK. Shane and I did a little detective work the last two days. These are the people you should contact.' He handed her a scribbled note. 'The questions are listed for each.'

'What's my job in all this?' July asked.

'It is a rarity for a woman to have a position of authority in this kind of inquiry,' Jared replied. 'So Wendy will pretend to be your assistant. You will have to ask the questions.'

'Me?'

'Wendy hardly set foot out of the hotel when she was here last, and then she was decked out like a rich wife, looking to get rid of her husband. No one should recognize her. However, some of us Valerons are known hereabouts; we needed someone not connected to the ranch. If anyone should recognize you, it's a simple task to tell them you landed the job when you lost your mining investment.'

July put on an unfaltering expression. 'I'll sure do my best, Mr Valeron.'

'My father is Mister Valeron,' Jared reminded him. With a smirk, 'You can call me . . . *sir*.'

That lightened the mood and everyone laughed.

Then the four of them sat down — three on the bed and July on the only chair — and began to discuss what they needed to do.

* * *

Rocco entered the ranch house, walked over to the kitchen counter and poured himself a drink from the half-empty whiskey bottle. Mantee was in the next room, sitting in an easy chair with a

Police Gazette magazine lying across his lap. He had been drinking a warm beer but set it down when his hired man arrived.

'What did you find out?' he asked Rocco.

'It's bad, boss,' the slender man said. 'One of the men is sure enough Jared Valeron — Rex recognized him. I double-checked — went by the newspaper office and looked at the picture of him and Wyatt Valeron, from the news story about the killers they brought in a few months back.'

'Where are the two morons who got us into this mess?'

'I left them to keep watch in town. I don't see Valeron and his pard as being too much of a threat by themselves. Fact is, the guy with him is maybe in his early twenties and looks more like a regular horse wrangler than an able gunman like Jared or Wyatt. There is enough similarity betwixt them, the two might be cousins or brothers. Don't know about that.'

'Damn!' Mantee grunted his concern. 'I'll have to let Pegg know.'

'We should be in the clear. I see the thirty head of cattle are here from that rancher over at Raccoon Creek. If they come snooping, seeing a few beef should be enough to make it look like we're running a small ranch.'

'Unless they already checked our place out. Remember, if they somehow managed to follow the stolen beef, they came in from the west. They might have looked us over when they arrived in the valley.'

Rocco frowned. 'We only held the Double B cattle overnight. And now we've got enough cattle for a good bluff.'

'Using a running iron to alter the brands on a few cattle isn't enough. Look at this place — no cut grass for winter feed, a rundown barn, half the fences falling down — how the hell is it supposed to pass for an honest-to-goodness ranch?'

Rocco ducked his head under the verbal assault. 'Me and the boys can put in a little hard labor. It shouldn't take but a few days to get it in shape.'

'First thing in the morning ride in and bring those two idiots back. Stick them on mending fences and we'll all pitch in to fix this place up to look like a working ranch.'

Rocco finished his drink and set the glass down. 'You got it, boss. I'll hit the sack and ride out at first light.'

* * *

Jared and Shane left the hotel and purposely ambled down the main street. The livery sat on the outskirts of town, due to the smell and noise from the blacksmith work. They were a few steps away from the perimeter corral when two men appeared from out of the shadows.

Both had their guns out and pointed at the two Valerons.

'Hold it!' one of the phantoms demanded. 'Reach for your hog-legs and we'll fill you full of lead!'

'Holy Hanna!' Shane whispered to Jared. 'I thought we were going to set a trap *for them*!'

'Rex and Dekay,' Jared spoke an easy greeting, lifting his hands a few inches above his shoulders, palms outward, posing no imminent threat. 'What have you boys been up to since you left the Barrett ranch?'

Rex's wicked grin was visible in the gloom. 'Reckon you know what we've been up to — seeing as how you followed us clean across the country.'

'Don't know what you're talking about,' Jared said, keeping his voice casual, prepared to react instantly if the chance arose. 'Me and my cousin just arrived in town to look over a couple of Hereford bulls. You know they are the future of the cattle industry, being much more hearty than the range cattle we have now. More meat on their bones too.'

'That why you were checking the tannery?' Dekay mocked the explanation. 'What do they offer a couple of would-be bull buyers?'

'Curiosity,' Jared answered easily. 'Shane here wanted to have a look at the beamhouse operations.'

Rex guffawed his disbelief. 'Sure. You wouldn't go there during the day and get a personal tour, would you? Better to sneak in at night.'

'Why the guns, boys?' Jared maintained an innocent persona. 'We didn't have nothing to do with your being let go from the ranch. That was Miss Barrett's decision.'

'Let's take a walk,' Rex ordered, waving the muzzle of his gun in the direction of the empty field beyond the livery. 'No need waking the whole town by talking too loud.'

Jared knew the talking would be with their guns. To go peacefully was to end up dead. All the same, he needed a split-second diversion to get his gun in play. Better to let them think they were going without a fuss.

'You know enough about us,' Shane spoke up to warn the two men. 'If you kill us, our family will hunt you down and put you both in the ground.'

'They ain't gonna know who killed

you,' Dekay spoke up.

'I'm afraid you're a little too late on that count,' Jared told them. 'I already sent a letter to my Pa and told him you two were involved. Your only chance is to grab your steeds and head for Mexico. For rustling cattle and killing a hired hand, they might not follow you across the border.'

'Jared's telling the truth,' Shane joined in. 'The one man you shot is a friend of ours, but he is going to pull through. He is the only reason we came looking for you. Kill us and you won't find a safe haven in the entire world.'

'Guess we'll have to take our chances, seeing as how — '

'Stop where you are!' a voice commanded from out of the darkness.

7

Dekay and Rex reacted at once, spinning around to shoot at whoever had given the command. Jared recognized the voice and sprang into action. He knew his life and Shane's were on the line so he didn't hesitate.

Dekay got off a round at a shadowy figure some thirty feet away. However, the lone man had dropped to a prone position rather than return fire.

Jared's gun sounded and Dekay grunted from twin slugs passing through his back and out his chest. Before he even staggered from the gunshots, Rex was also hit twice. He had been slow to react and didn't manage to get off a shot before the rustler was dead on his feet. He sank straight down to flop into an awkward sitting position. His head rolled forward and he toppled over with his face in the dirt. Dekay remained on his feet long enough to twist his body around to glare back at Jared. Then his legs lost their resiliency and he slumped down alongside his partner in crime, eyes staring sightless in death.

Shane had not even gotten his gun clear before the short fight was over.

Jared kept his gun trained on the two rustlers but knew they were finished. He walked past them and stared at the man who had rescued them.

'Colby! You hit?'

July rose up to his feet and began to walk toward them. He hadn't even drawn a weapon. 'No sir,' he answered. 'I saw you still had your gun, and both you and Shane were directly in line with the two gunmen. I didn't dare take a shot for fear of hitting one of you. I just hollered and hit the dirt.' He stopped to brush the dust off of his shirt and pants, then shook his head in awe. 'Them two never had a chance against you. Durned if you ain't as quick and deadly as a bolt of lightning!'

Jared holstered his weapon, moved the remaining distance to July and shook his hand. 'You can forget calling me sir. I'm Jared to you from now on,' he said. 'Don't know how you got here, but you sure enough saved our hides.'

'We forgot to ask where you were staying,' July clarified his presence. 'Miss Valeron asked me to catch up with you so we would know . . . in case there was trouble.' He tipped his head toward the two dead men. 'That's when I spotted these two sidewinders following you. When they took off running down an alleyway, it occurred to me they were going to get ahead of you. Didn't seem any logic to that unless they intended to bushwhack you. I stayed out of sight until they started to herd you out of town.'

'They wanted us far enough away so the sound of the shots wouldn't bring the police.'

Shane grunted a warning. 'Speaking of the local law enforcement, I see a couple of them headed this way.'

'Saves us the trouble of rounding them up,' Jared said. 'We'll clear this up tonight and get a good night's sleep.'

Then speaking to July, 'Don't tell these guys you work at our ranch. Just say you saw two men stalking us from your hotel window and came to warn us.'

'I catch your drift,' July said. 'I was just being a good citizen.'

Jared raised his hands to show the lawmen he didn't have a ready weapon. Shane did likewise, while July stepped away from them, backing up a few steps.

As the pair of officers arrived, the older one took charge. He was medium height, but had girth from his years, probably close to forty. He displayed a grave expression, accentuated by a thick mustache that appeared to be the pride of his face. He looked over the two bodies, but it took no medical skills to see the pair had departed this world. Finally, he scrutinized Jared and Shane.

'I'm Officer Fielding,' he informed the group. 'And I've had a run-in a time or two with these pokes around town. They sometimes work out at the Big M ranch for Pierce Mantee.'

'Wouldn't know about that,' Jared

informed him. 'They used to work at the Barrett ranch some months back. After my family helped to get the place back for Miss Barrett, they were fired for being in cahoots with the woman and her outlaw kid — the ones who poisoned Mr Barrett and tried to steal the place from Trina Barrett.'

'You're one of them Valerons who brought in those three killers!' the other policeman exclaimed. 'Sure! I remember.' He laughed. 'Never seen the like — three men with ropes around their necks, like some kind of ghoulish carnival entering town.'

Jared grinned. 'As Cousin Wyatt was with me, I'm afraid that was a little bit like showing off. But it was necessary when I had been handling them by myself.'

'And what's the deal about these two? Were they getting even with you for being fired?'

'Something like that. They were herding us out of town, so no one would hear the gunshots, when this feller shouted at them to stop.'

Fielding turned to look at July. 'What's your story, mister?'

'I seen two sneaky-looking characters trailing along behind these two,' he explained. 'I didn't know what it was about, but I felt it was my civic duty to check and see.'

'And who are you?'

'July Colby,' he answered. 'I'm working for the governor at the moment, doing some research around town.' He took a moment to remove the introductory paper from his shirt pocket and handed it to Fielding. As the officer looked over the document, he finished his story. 'Anyhow, when I seen these two get the drop on these two fellows, I shouted at them to stop. They both swung around to shoot at me, so I made like a mole and burrowed into the ground.' He made a helpless gesture. 'I'm not much good with a gun.'

Fielding handed back the paper and looked at Jared. 'And you did the rest?'

'I drilled them both, before they could get off more than one shot at him or turn their guns on us,' Jared replied. 'If you check all of the weapons, you'll discover Dekay got off one round, and my Colt has four empties. I put two bullets in each man.'

Fielding bobbed his head. 'We heard the shooting — sounded like a string of firecrackers going off.'

Jared lifted his shoulders in a shrug. 'I didn't want to take a chance with them. One quick desperation shot might have killed one of us.'

'You'll have to appear before a judge tomorrow,' Fielding said professionally. 'It's customary for us to hold a suspect in jail until they are cleared of any wrongdoing.' He let the notion hang in the air for a moment. Then he relaxed. 'But seeing as how we know you personally, Mr Valeron, I'll take your word. Be at the courthouse at ten in the morning, so we can get this settled and done with.'

'We appreciate the courtesy, Officer Fielding,' Jared replied to the order. 'Shane and I will be there.' He jerked a thumb at July. 'You want this alert stranger here to tell his story too?'

'He's working for the governor,' Fielding dismissed the idea. 'Me and Sam got his statement. That should be good enough. I'll report to my superiors, but I think McEnroe and the captain will be satisfied.'

'Thank you,' July said. 'I only did what any citizen should do.' Then, flashing his easy smile. 'I'm just glad Mr Valeron here is a good shot. I was lying there, exposed like a wounded deer, hunkered down trying to make myself as small a target as possible.'

'You saved the lives of these two men. Thanks for lending a hand.' Fielding told July. Then, directing his words at the Valeron boys, 'Let's get these two bodies off of the street. We can put them inside the livery until I round up the undertaker.'

* * *

Wendy was at the hotel entrance as July came walking back up the street. She had heard the shooting and raced down from her room to see what had happened.

'July!' she cried out. 'Is everything all right?'

He hurried his step, jogging the last little way, not saying a word until he reached her. Then he pulled her off to the side, back in the darker shadows and away from any other curious spectators that had gathered along the street.

'It's OK, Miss Valeron,' he assured her. Then he explained about seeing the two men following after Jared and Shane. He related how the gunfight had come about and ended by telling her about the two lawmen.

Wendy stared at him as if he had grown a second head. 'July!' she declared. 'You could have been killed!'

He grinned. 'I admit to being a little worried when I called out at those two bushwhackers, but your brother sure lived up to your bragging. Never seen a man so quick to react. Them two only got off one shot betwixt them, before Jared downed them both . . . deader'n a couple rocks.'

'But what if Jared had been a little slow?'

He frowned. 'I hit the ground like a dropped watermelon, Miss Valeron. Once I seen Jared and Shane still had their guns, I only drew the attention of them two outlaws. I figured your brother would take care of them and he sure enough did.'

Casting aside propriety, Wendy threw her arms around July and hugged him. 'You saved their lives!' she exclaimed, her lips next to his ear. 'You risked your own life to save theirs.'

July was caught flat-footed by her emotional hug, but he took advantage of her reaction. His arms went around her and he held her tight. Wendy remained in his grasp for a few seconds, trying to regain her aplomb. When she had recovered, she removed her hands from his back and he quickly took a step back.

To hide her embarrassment over such a gushing display, she smiled up at him. 'Goes to show, a person doesn't have to be good with a gun to save a man's life.'

July laughed. 'Yeah, so long as that man is Jared . . . and he still has his gun. I reckon we'd all three be dead had Jared not been armed.'

'Daddy didn't hire you to be a gun-hand.'

'Actually, I kind of figured your daddy only hired me because of you. You're the one who got me and T L on the Barrett payroll.'

'Best thing I ever did,' Wendy told him. 'And, about now, I'm sure Jerry is glad he went along with the idea.'

'Winning your brother over is sure worth risking my life.'

'Yes, but dying in the process would make it all quite pointless!' she scolded him. 'Don't you ever do something so all fired crazy again.'

'No, Miss Valeron,' he promised, 'I won't.'

'And the name is Wendy. You earned that liberty by your actions.' She smiled at him. 'And Jerry will for sure back me up about that!'

'You bet, Miss Val- uh,' he quickly

made the correction, '. . . Miss Wendy. I'll treasure the honor.'

Wendy heaved a final sigh, ending their jocularity. 'Now that we've got everything settled for the night, would you please escort me to my room? We need to try and get a few hours rest before we start our interviews tomorrow.'

'Proud to escort you, Miss Wendy,' July said, displaying an unusual boldness. 'Proud as one of them there peacocks!'

* * *

Mantee had put Jones and Squint to work on the corral. He chose to sweep out the house and make it more presentable, in case anyone showed up to check out the ranch. The powdery particulates rose up until he could hardly see or breathe as he pushed the pile of debris out the front door. He was swatting at the irksome heap, knocking it off the porch, when Rocco came thundering into the yard.

The man pulled his mount to a jerky

stop, causing a renewed cloud of dust. His poor horse was lathered and heaving from a hard run.

'Damn, Rocco!' Mantee growled. 'What's the idea? You trying to kill that animal!'

'They're both dead!' Rocco snarled his mixture of anger and fear. 'The Valerons killed Rex and Dekay last night!'

'What?' Mantee howled in alarm. 'How the devil did that happen?'

Squint and Jones had ceased their chores and hurried over to see what Rocco's rush was all about. They shared Mantee's alarm at the news.

'They's both dead?' Squint repeated inanely. 'Them two was only supposed to keep an eye on what was happening.'

'Spill it!' Mantee bid Rocco continue.

'It seems the two dummies tried to get rid of the Valerons before they come looking for us,' Rocco outlined what he had learned. 'Near as I could tell talking to the newspaper hound — he'd just come from speaking to one of the police — Rex and Dekay were herding the Valerons out of town to shoot them. Some passerby gent shouted at them . . . ' Rocco lifted his hands in a helpless gesture. 'That's all it took. Valeron drew down on them and kilt them both deader than your boot leather. There's gonna be a hearing about the shooting at ten this morning.'

'Of all the stupid . . . ' Mantee didn't finish, swearing vehemently instead. 'This ain't good.'

'You think them Valerons will come out here?' Squint asked. 'Once they know those two were working for us, it's what I would do.'

'We do have a bit of wiggle room,' Rocco suggested. The other three men waited for him to explain. 'What I'm saying, those two were fired from the Barrett spread. They blamed the Valerons for ruining the easy life they had — being they were working with Rob and his mother. This don't have to look like anything more than simple revenge on their part.'

'Unless they opened their big mouths about our operation,' Mantee replied.

Rocco shook his head. 'With them two dead, they have no evidence against us. Pegg and Hank Grubber covered our tracks — no cattle and no hides. We are in the clear.'

'What about the killing of those two men on the Double B spread?' Jones asked the question. 'The Valerons are not gonna let this go until they get their pound of flesh.'

'It was Rex and Dekay — they stole the beef,' Rocco maintained. 'They did the killing. We only used them on occasion, when we needed help rounding up or driving cattle.'

Mantee rubbed his hands together. 'I like your thinking, Rocco. No matter what them two were guilty of, we can claim we didn't know nothing about it.'

''Cause they was only sometime help!' Squint also joined in on the alibi. 'Sure! We got nothing to fear. We keep working the ranch like we're serious until them boys consider their vendetta over and done with.'

'No proof, no evidence, no need for

them to stick around,' Jones also confirmed the idea.

Mantee gave the notion a little thought. The others waited for their leader to make his decision. Finally, he tipped his head in an affirmative bob.

'Here's what we do, men. I've got the perfect cover and it gets all of us off the hook.' He explained what he had in mind, then looked at Rocco.

'Get yourself a fresh horse. Ride over to Pegg's and pass the word to him and Hank. I'll head for town and be at the hearing. With our story in place, ain't no one going to point a finger at any of us.'

Rocco left the room and Mantee looked at Jones. 'Didn't you say you knew one of the men that Valeron brought in to be hanged — was it Kidd?'

'Yeah, I did some small-time rustling with the Kidd brothers back a few years, before I joined up with you.'

'Tim died at the end of a rope — but you knew his brother?'

'Meaner than a rabid dog — Dixon Kidd, Tim's older brother. He got stuck in the hoosegow for carving up a deputy in Pueblo. He was serving his time when Valeron brought in Kidd and those others to be hanged.'

'But he's out now?'

'A couple months back,' Jones gave a nod. 'I believe he took up with a couple no-accounts what used to run with Crazy Calhoun's gang. You remember Calhoun was killed during a bank holdup last year.'

'Do you think you could get hold of him?'

'Dixon Kidd?'

'Yes,' Mantee said. 'He might like the idea of a little payback for Valeron getting his brother hanged.'

Jones skewed a thoughtful expression. 'Dix used to work out of a backwater saloon over at Eagle Point. It's not more than a full day's ride. I'll send a wire and see if he's close by.' With a narrow look, 'What's your thinking?'

'Let's call it a secondary plan, just in case the Valerons stick around. We don't need them looking over our shoulder or snooping into our operation.'

'I get it,' Jones said. 'If your first plan don't work, it'd be a sight better if someone besides us did away with Valeron.'

'My thinking exactly. Ride into town and send the message.'

8

Wendy gave July a subtle wink for confidence as they entered Stanley's Meat Market. The shop was quite small, but had a glass-front counter, allowing the customer to see his display of meats. Stanley was a middle-aged man, with short hair and a bald spot on the top of his head. He carried some extra weight around his middle, but displayed an instant smile that looked more genuine than professional.

'Good morning, folks!' he greeted them warmly. 'Don't recall seeing you in my humble store before. Welcome.'

'It's very nice for a butcher shop,' Wendy told him, making a short survey of the room. 'Much cleaner than most.'

He chuckled. 'That's because most of my customers are women, young lady. They do most of the family shopping — the *meat* of my business, you might say.' He laughed.

'That's one of them there puns.'

'Very witty,' Wendy smiled at his efforts.

'What can I do for you?' He asked. 'I've got these fresh fryers here' — he pointed to three plucked chickens — 'or a nice pork roast. Always have bacon or salt pork available in the back room too.'

'Chickens look fresh,' July spoke up for the first time, looking through the glass case. 'But I don't see much beef.'

'Oh, I carry a full array of steaks, roasts, or stew meat,' Stanley informed him. 'But I only put out a sample or two. Most people order it in advance. Beef is quite expensive directly from the local shops.'

'That so?' July continued on the line. 'Why is that?'

'Well, we have a sizable slaughterhouse outside of town that deals mostly in beef. They sell to everyone in the city, also to the mines, the restaurants, and about every other buyer for miles around. They also sell to us local store owners, but we can't compete with them when it comes to selling more than an occasional cut of meat. I rarely have more than a quarter-beef hanging in the back room. Even then, I often take a loss to get rid of some of it.'

'But the individual buyer . . .' July began.

Stanley held up a hand to stop the question. 'I get a commission for handling the slaughterhouse sales. I take orders for the meat from my regular customers and pass it on to Singeon Pegg — he owns the meat-packing company. Anyway, I get their order the next day and the shopper gets a better price than I could give them. Don't know how he does it, but my cost is about what those people get their meat for. Can't compete with that.'

'Sounds like he would put a small place out of business,' July said.

'You've hit the spike squarely on the head, friend. It's the reason I sell mostly pork, mutton and chicken.'

July remarked, 'You must have some idea about how he keeps his price low enough to undercut you and any other store owners.'

Stanley threw a suspicious look at both July and Wendy. 'I've got to ask, what is the purpose of your visit? I mean, you two don't strike me as a couple aiming to buy a pound of ground beef.'

'Actually,' July fielded the question, 'we have been commissioned to study the different commercial enterprises in Denver.' At the man's surprised look, he explained. 'You see, the governor wants to draw in more businesses, without bringing in competition for people like you, the current local business owners.'

'We are doing a survey,' Wendy contributed, flashing an approving glance at July for his flawless delivery. 'It will help the governor promote Denver as a good place to start new companies — yet protect those of you who are already established.'

'Sounds like a smart idea,' Stanley approved. 'Was I wanting to know anything about the slaughterhouse, I'd visit Don Larson. He tried to make a go of a meat market a year or so back. Ended up working for Pegg cutting and wrapping meat.' He gave a firm bob of his head. 'Tell you straight, Larson is a first-rate meat cutter. Since he started working there, I've never had a complaint from anyone about him leaving anything on the bone a buyer wouldn't want to pay for. He trims every cut purty as you please.'

July asked for directions to his house and thanked him for his input. Once he and Wendy were back out on the walk, he let out the breath he'd been holding.

'Whew!' he panted. 'Glad that is over.'

'You did fine,' Wendy praised his work. 'You didn't miss a word or say one wrong thing.'

He grunted. 'Yeah, because I had you to fill in the blank spots and do much of the talking.'

'We make a good team,' she said cheerfully. 'We are going to have to rent a buggy. The man he told us about — that Larson fellow — sounds like the one we need to talk to.'

'You bet. If he was run out of business by this Pegg character, he ought to be willing to spill whatever beans he knows about.'

'First off, July, I'm not used to sleeping late and missing breakfast. It's time for something to eat. How about you take me someplace nice?'

'I don't have but a couple dollars.'

She laughed. 'Silly! Daddy is paying for everything.'

'In that case, Miss Valeron, you can pick out whichever eatery you want.'

* * *

The court hearing was attended by a lone clerk, the judge, Police Officer Fielding and his immediate supervisor — a short, but sturdy-looking man he introduced as Sergeant McEnroe — plus Shane and Jared. However, there was one surprise visitor, a man who owned a nearby ranch. As soon as the clerk announced the reason for the hearing, the gent stood up and asked the judge for permission to speak.

'We're looking into a simple gunfight,' the judge told him. 'Does this have relevance to the deaths of Rex Anderson and Orion Dekay?'

'It does.'

'Proceed,' he allowed. 'State your name and speak your piece.'

'I'm Pierce Mantee, owner of the Big M ranch, about ten miles west of Denver,' the man began. 'As for them two fellers, I'd like to state they sometimes worked for me — usually when I had a roundup or cattle drive lined up. They didn't live at the ranch, but they were usually around when we needed help.'

'You said this had relevance?' the judge prompted him to get to the point.

'Yes, Your Honor,' Mantee replied. 'Them two come by a week or so ago, wanting to sell me fifty head of steers. They claimed to have bought them real cheap, but I seen the brand — the Double B — and I knew the Barrett ranch didn't sell cattle that way.' He snorted his disdain. 'I told them I didn't want no part of stolen beef and sent them on down the road. They headed off in the direction of Pueblo.'

'And why is this relevant to this hearing?'

'Like I said, them two worked for me on occasion, and I knew about their personal grudge against the Valerons. They blamed them for losing their jobs at the Double B. I thought you ought to know about that. It shows that there thing called motive, meaning they had a reason to want to get even with the Valerons. I reckon they were the ones responsible for this here row.'

The judge waved a hand. 'Thank you, Mr Mantee,' he said. 'The court appreciates your coming forward with this information.'

Mantee had said what he intended. He thanked the judge for listening to what he had to say and left the courtroom.

Officer Fielding was the next to give his account, summing up what had taken place. Then the judge asked Jared a question or two, learning about the stolen cattle and the murder of one of the

Double B hands. He finished by directing his attention to McEnroe.

'Are you satisfied with the explanations and outcome of this encounter, sergeant?'

'The captain has signed off on the death of the two men as self-defense, Your Honor,' McEnroe reported. 'The evidence and witnesses all support the scene as we found it.'

'That being the case,' the judge declared, 'no charges will be forthcoming. I hereby declare the shooting was in self-defense. This court is adjourned.'

Fielding and McEnroe left with Jared and Shane, then stopped to talk to them outside the courthouse.

'This killing you spoke of to the judge, out at the Double B,' McEnroe inquired. 'That's the same shooting that put Mr Dodge in the local hospital?'

Jared told him what they had learned and their tracking the cattle to the slaughterhouse.

'Mantee said them two headed the herd for Pueblo,' McEnroe clarified.

'But you say the trail ended at Pegg's slaughterhouse?'

'That's right.'

'Yet you found nothing to prove anything against Pegg?'

'They covered their tracks right quick,' Jared said. 'Butchered the cattle and got rid of the hides before we could track them down.'

Fielding sighed. 'We've been a little curious about how Pegg manages to undercut every other outlet of beef. He had a special sale just the other day, selling some prime beef at a real discount. My wife got us a roast and several steaks for about half the usual price.' He scowled from his suspicions. 'I have to believe there's a good chance that's where the Double B steers ended up.'

'But there's no proof of wrongdoing,' McEnroe complained. 'The two men who likely brought the cattle to the slaughterhouse are dead.'

Fielding bobbed his head in agreement with his sergeant. 'We can't post a man to watch them every day, and there's no telling how often Pegg buys a few head of rustled cattle.'

'We know what we're up against,' Jared said, displaying a wry grimace. 'But we intend to do a little more snooping. If we uncover anything, we'll let you know before we hang anyone.'

McEnroe laughed. 'Yeah, our captain and the judge both take a dim view of hangings without due process.'

'Cousin Jared always gives them due process,' Shane quipped. 'After they confess, he gives them five minutes to pray for their souls . . . before he hangs them.'

The two lawmen grinned at the remark and Fielding lifted his hand in farewell. As the two men walked away, Shane turned to Jared.

'Now what?'

'Guess we'll give Wendy and July a day or two to do their job. If they come up empty, we will take a more direct approach.'

'How about us? What do we do until then?'

'Let's check on Dodge, then ride out

and spend the day with Pa. I'll ride back and visit Wendy tomorrow and see how things are going. You've earned a day off.'

'No argument from me. That cheap room you rented has harder beds than the ground we've been sleeping on for the past week.'

* * *

It was something of a surprise to find Don Larson at his home. His wife answered the door, a matronly, though still attractive woman with laugh lines about her eyes and a ready smile. She greeted July and Wendy as if they were dear friends and invited them into her house. Don entered the family room as they sat down side by side on a worn, but comfortable sofa.

'We don't get many visitors this far out of town,' Gayle said, after handing each of them a glass of lemonade. 'Donny has been working a lot of extra hours so this week Mr Pegg is balancing the scales.'

'Cheaper than adding up all of the

hours and paying me extra,' Don added with a grin.

'We don't want to take a lot of your time,' July told them. 'Hate to intrude on anything special you have planned.'

'What brings you out here to see me?' Don asked them.

July explained they were auditors from the governor's office, researching the beef industry from source to market.

'We were told you were an honest man,' Wendy jumped in. 'It's why we chose to speak to you first.'

'First?'

'You may not be aware of it,' she continued, 'but over five hundred head of cattle have been misappropriated in eastern Colorado during the past eighteen months. On the surface, twenty-five to thirty head of cattle disappearing each month is not a huge amount. However, the smaller ranchers are struggling to survive and a couple are failing due to these losses.'

'What does this have to do with Donny?' his wife asked, her concern shining in her eyes.

July put forth an austere aspect. 'We heard talk that the slaughterhouse where you work . . . uh' — he searched for the proper word — '*processed* a large number of beef within the past ten days.'

'Why should that matter?' Don asked.

Wendy was quick to respond. 'We spoke to a couple of range detectives. They claimed to have tracked a small herd of misappropriated cattle to your work place.'

Don frowned, suddenly wary, though he didn't become hostile. 'We did handle a fairly large number of beef in the last ten days. As to an actual count or where they came from, I have no idea.'

'You didn't get a look at them when they were in the holding corral?' July wanted to know. 'Perhaps saw what brand they were carrying?'

'I glanced out the back door the day they arrived and was surprised to see the pen was full to overflowing,' he admitted. 'But I never concern myself with brands or such. I couldn't tell you anything about them other than they were prime beef. That much I know from cutting and packaging the meat.'

'Don only sees a side of beef at a time,' Gayle stated. 'His work all comes from the meat locker, after the cattle have been dressed and hung on meat hooks.'

Wendy took on a serious, yet understanding look. 'We are not making charges against anyone for any crime,' she assured the couple. 'However, two men attempted to kill those range detectives last night, and we're pretty sure the two culprits had a connection to where you work.'

'Connection? Who were they?' Don wanted to know. 'There's only a half-dozen of us working full time.'

'The names of the two men were Rex Anderson and Orion Dekay.'

'Pierce Mantee's men!' Don said, not hiding his distaste. 'The two of them helped Everett with the skinning and then took the hides to the tannery. Everett mentioned their names when complaining to me how little help they were.'

'How about this Everett?' July asked.

'Any chance he would tell us about the brands on those cattle?'

'I don't know. He isn't much for talking. He has been working for Pegg and his father for the past half-dozen years.'

'Would you expect him to be a part of any misappropriation of cattle?' Wendy put forth the question.

'Everett is a working fool. He does a job very few men would want. He doesn't complain about the pay — and I suspect he will be guarded about saying anything bad about either Singeon or Bingham Pegg. Other than slaughterhouse work I can't think of one other job he would be qualified for.'

'So it's a father-and-son business?' Wendy asked.

'Bingham is pretty much retired. He did come in to help with the meat cutting, but he turned the place over to his son a couple years ago. The old man isn't much of a talker, but he did say he was amazed at how his son had been able to turn a much better profit than he ever did.'

'We were told Pegg ran you out of business,' Wendy changed the subject. 'That would be Singeon?'

'Yeah, he undercut our prices when we refused his offer to sell his beef on a commission basis.' Don grunted. 'Worse, as I had no facilities to butcher my own beef, we were forced to buy most of the meat from him to start with. He doesn't do only wholesale like most slaughter-houses, he also does retail. He sells to practically every outlet in the valley — that's what my job is, the cutting and packaging of those orders.'

'Stanley, from the little shop in town, told us a little about it. He said the profit for his store came mostly from chicken and pork, because he couldn't compete with the prices of the slaughterhouse on beef.' Wendy smiled. 'He's the one who told us you were an honest man.'

'He can afford to be generous now,' Gayle complained. 'When we opened up our store, he was not so kind with his words.'

'Because you were in competition

with him,' July postulated. 'Now he can tell the truth about you.'

'If Mr Pegg is involved in something illegal,' Gayle appeared worried, 'will that mean Donny might lose his job?'

'The need for beef won't change in the valley,' July said. 'There has to be a slaughterhouse to handle the demand. It's them cattle which are miss-propriated that we're concerned about.'

Wendy flicked a glance at him and July flinched, knowing he had misused a word and used poor grammar in his delivery. However, the Larsons didn't appear to notice.

'Everett's place is north of here about a mile. He's married to a gal who was widowed during the Indian wars. She had a couple kids and he needed a housekeeper. She and her kids attend church regularly, but Everett doesn't want to give up his one day off a week. He mostly goes fishing on our usual day off.'

'We're much obliged to you for speaking to us,' July said. 'And thank you kindly for the lemonade. It was real good.'

Wendy rose to her feet with July. 'Yes, we would appreciate your not speaking of our visit or purpose, Mr and Mrs Larson. The range detectives' investigation is ongoing, and it might be some time before they reach any conclusions.'

'And if they find Pegg is buying stolen beef?' Don wanted to know.

'It's like we first advised you, the need for the slaughterhouse will remain. If Mr Pegg should be involved and charged with a crime, I'm sure he will appoint someone to keep his business going. If not, I know of a small town that could use a good meat-cutter. It would mean moving some distance, but it's a very nice place for raising children.'

'Let's hope it doesn't come to that,' Gayle said. 'We're quite happy here.'

'We will have to see what the future has in store for all of us,' Wendy offered. 'Thank you so much for speaking to us.'

* * *

Pegg frowned, reading the dispatch that had arrived by a town courier. The news was not good. He paced the room for a bit and then called Louie in from where he had been sweeping floors.

'What's up, Mr Pegg?' Louie asked.

Louie was twenty years old and a hard worker. He had been raised by a strict father and did not question any order given to him. Everett would sometimes tease the young man, but Louie had no temper. He was about as easygoing as a dandelion.

'I've a couple errands for you to run.'

'Sure thing, Mr Pegg. Whatever you need.'

'Ride over to Everett's place and tell him to be watchful for any strangers who might come nosing about. Any questions about our operation, he is to refer them to me.'

'OK.'

'Then run out to the Big M and speak to Pierce Mantee,' Pegg instructed. 'Tell him I would like to see him this afternoon.'

'Sure thing, Mr Pegg,' Louie replied. 'You want I should tell him the same as Everett?'

'No, he knows how to handle snoops. Just tell him I want a word with him.'

'How about Don Larson?'

Pegg didn't want to raise an alarm and he knew from experience that Don never looked at the live cattle. Some men were like that — once the animal was butchered, they could dice and slice and cut meat from calf, lamb or fawns, but they didn't want to see the critter beforehand. It wasn't exactly a weakness, more of a desire to separate the living from the dead. He shook his head.

'Just what I've told you.'

'OK, Mr Pegg,' Louie accepted the orders. 'Talk to Everett, then tell Mr Mantee to come and see you.'

'Oh, and Louie?' Pegg stopped him before he could get out the door. The young man looked over his shoulder, waiting. 'If anyone should ask you about your job here, about what we do, anything at all . . . you refer them to me. Understand?'

'You don't want me to talk to no strangers about my job or anything to do with this place.'

'That's it exactly.'

'You can trust me, Mr Pegg. I won't tell anybody nuthen about nuthen.'

'Good boy,' Pegg praised him.

Louie stood poised, waiting, in case Pegg had anything else to tell him. When he waved his hand in a dismissing gesture, the young man went out the door.

Next thing, Pegg visited Ingram, who was dumping fat into a cooking vat. He had dozens of tubs waiting to be processed. His two helpers were busy straining and using containers for the previous batch. The room smelled like old guts, combined with the greasy smell of fat. Rather than call him away from his duties, Pegg walked over to stand next to him.

'Anyone been out to your place to visit you lately?' he asked the man.

'Not a soul,' Ingram replied. 'Why?'

'There's some people snooping around — I think they are looking for a reason to shut us down or maybe add some new tax to our operation.'

'Never knew we had any problems with taxes or competition.'

'Well, the governor is behind it, so I suspect he's looking for ways to add more money to his budget.'

Ingram snorted. 'Just what we need . . . more government sticking their noses into our business.'

Pegg bobbed his head in agreement. 'Well, I wanted you to know, in case some people showed up at your door.'

'I'll run 'em off with my scatter-gun!'

Pegg raised his hands in a calming gesture. 'I don't think you need take it that far, Gabe. Just don't give them any information about the how or why we do things the way we do — give them nothing about the cattle we process or our operation here. If they want questions answered, they can darn well talk to me.'

'OK, Pegg,' Ingram said. 'I'll give them the time of day and send them on their way.' He grinned. 'Hey! That there rhymes, don't it?'

'You ought to write it down. Who knows, you might take up writing poetry when you retire from real work.'

'Yeah. That'll be the day.'

'See you later,' Pegg said and left the room. He had begun to sweat from simply being in the same room as their rendering process, but it brought in a lot of added revenue. A pound of tallow was currently selling for more than a pound of beef. Who would have ever thought that could happen?

9

Mantee shook hands with Dixon Kidd. He paused as Kidd introduced the two scroungy-looking men with him. He offered only a single name for each — Ponce and Victor — before the four of them went into the house. He poured the visitors a glass of whiskey each and they all sat down at the kitchen table.

'I was sorry to hear about your brother,' Mantee opened the conversation. 'Those Valerons are a menace to anyone in our line of work.'

'You said there was a chance to get even,' Kidd was blunt. 'That's why we're here.'

'Job pays five hundred dollars,' Mantee told him. 'And all you have to do is kill Jared Valeron and the man riding with him.'

Kidd grunted. 'I'd have come here and killed Valeron for nothing.' He hooked a thumb at his two men. 'Howsome-whatsoever, my boys like to spend big when we are flush, so we will be happy to take your money.'

Mantee put on a sympathetic mien. 'Tell you the truth, I was surprised they hanged every one of them boys. According to the testimony I read about, there was no proof given that they had ever killed anyone.'

'Considering their history and wanted posters, then showing the judge and jury those two dummies shot full of holes . . . ' Kidd shrugged. 'It was enough proof that got them hanged.'

'Yeah, with one of the forms being made up to look like a bride-to-be, I can see how that would look pretty bad.'

'So, you got a plan, Mantee?' Kidd wanted to know. 'Or are you gonna point a direction and let us go find those two on our own?'

'I'd like for you to sit tight a day or two. Singeon Pegg calls the shots on this job, but it's for certain we're gonna take care of the two Valerons that showed up. The boss has worked out a plan so that none of us will have to worry about getting caught.'

'That's the kind of plan I like best,' Kidd agreed. 'So long as we get to do the job we came for.'

'It ought to be a short wait,' Mantee assured him. 'Until then, you can bunk and eat with us. I'll let you know as soon as everything is ready. Just don't get too comfortable and don't drink too much. We'll need clear heads and quick action when the time comes.'

'We'll stick around for a couple days,' Kidd answered. 'But I intend to get the job done . . . with or without your help.'

* * *

Jared was waiting in July's room when he returned to the hotel for the night. The two of them went down the hall and joined Wendy. He listened while the two of them told him what they had learned.

'Did you speak to this Everett character?' Jared asked, when they had finished.

'He gave us nothing,' July answered. 'Get more answers from a fence post.'

'I'm guessing he was warned ahead of time,' Wendy opined.

Jared frowned at her. 'Do you think they got onto your game already?'

She displayed a puzzlement of her own. 'I can't imagine how. We only spoke to a couple store owners and the meat-cutter for the slaughterhouse. He seemed to share our concerns about how Pegg was able to control the price of beef in the area. And he told us Pegg senior had barely been making ends meet, before his son took over the place. Now it is turning a healthy profit."

'You think someone tipped them off?' July asked Jared. 'The meat-cutter is the only one we told about stolen beef and he promised to keep quiet about it.'

'Pa said there were still some crooked characters in power here in Denver. We will have to take that into account for any plan we come up with.'

'We did like you asked and didn't show up for the trial,' Wendy said. 'You were adamant about us keeping our distance from you and Shane.'

'I had every right to have been there,' July complained. 'We were worried you might get a judge who needed convincing about the facts of your case.'

'We had no trouble,' Jared dismissed his concern. 'And it's just as well you weren't there. A fellow named Pierce Mantee showed up from the Big M ranch. He told a wild tale about Rex and Dekay trying to dump the stolen cattle on him. Then he claimed they moved the herd in the direction of Pueblo.'

July laughed at the notion. 'Two guys? Stealing fifty head of cattle and driving them to the Utah border and back, then looking at another ninety miles of trail driving? I ain't no real cowpuncher yet, but even I say that's a load of slag.'

'I'm betting Mantee and his Big M ranch are a part of this rustling operation. We passed the place on our way to the slaughterhouse. The only sign of cattle on the place was a pasture close to the house . . . and the leavings were all fresh. Also, we didn't see signs of a remuda of horses, no feed, no decent fencing — nothing but a few horses in a rundown corral, and a dilapidated shack.'

'Have you got a plan lined out yet?' July asked.

'We turned over a few ideas with Reb and Pa, but the lack of evidence is going to be a challenge.'

'What do you need July and me to do?' Wendy wanted to know. 'If Everett was warned, none of Pegg's men are likely to give us any useful information.'

'You're right, sis. I think your visit to the slaughterhouse tomorrow will conclude that part of the plan. First, tell me about what you've learned,' he said, 'and don't leave anything out.'

* * *

The arrival of the two unknown people at the butchery was not a surprise, considering they had already been in contact with Larson and Everett. Pegg bid them enter his office, offered them a chair and sat down behind his desk.

Folding his arms, he leaned back and awaited their dialog.

'We are from the governor's office,' July began. He paused to hand over an official letter of introduction. 'As you can see, we have been given the authority to inspect the records of all businesses in the Denver region.'

'What kind of records?'

'Sales and receipt records,' July replied. 'If you would be so kind, we would like to see your ledger or journal containing your sales and purchases for the past two years right up to the present.' He waved a hand. 'It's to gauge whether or not all demands for beef are being met, and how well you can cope with increased demands. The governor is expecting considerable growth in the area.'

'I've had no complaints about having enough product on hand,' Pegg replied. 'And I pay a lot of money in taxes.'

'I'm sure you do,' July remained amicable. 'However, the governor has to con sider the city's future. The sales records?'

Pegg continued to grumble, but

opened his desk drawer and removed a thick accounting journal with a worn, tattered cover. He passed it to July, who handed it to Wendy. She opened the book and began to scan the pages.

'If you wouldn't mind,' July asked, 'I wonder if you would show me the operation? I've never actually been in a slaughterhouse before.'

'We prefer to call it a *meat processing plant*,' Pegg informed him curtly. 'We do have to butcher the animals here, but our more refined customers like to think of it as an industrial process.'

'I understand.'

Pegg shot a suspicious glance at Wendy, who was scribbling numbers on to a note-pad. He kept his temper in check and left the desk, leading the way out of the office.

While July kept him busy, Wendy rushed to copy down the totals — listing a tally of beef 'processed' for each month and year along with the total weights column. Next she recorded the sales figures. By the time the two men returned, she had jotted down all of the information she needed.

'Everything looks fine,' she spoke to Pegg, placing the ledger on his desk. 'I think we can safely tell the governor that Mr Pegg's operation can handle the flow of expected miners and new businesses in the Denver area.'

'His layout is impressive,' July remarked. 'I never knew how much there was to butchering . . . uh, *processing* beef. And his cold storage is something to see. Must be forty or more sides of beef hanging in that place.'

'If you are both quite finished here, I have orders to fill,' Pegg said a bit impatiently. 'Can't dally or gossip all day.'

'For sure,' July said. 'We will be on our way. Our job for the governor is pretty much wrapped up. You were our last stop.'

'Good.'

The two of them bid good day to Pegg and left the premises. Pegg wandered over to a window to watch their departure and made a decision. As soon as Mantee arrived, he would put a watchdog on those two. If they were finished, they should be returning to wherever they came from. If they ended up talking to the law, he would know about that too.

* * *

Aware of the fact the rustling and slaughterhouse ring knew his identity, Jared and Shane didn't hide their trip to visit Dodge. They rode in with Reb and discussed what they had learned with Dodge. He was feeling better and sitting up in bed. At learning Rex and Dekay had been behind the rustling he was livid. If they hadn't already been stowed six feet underground in their wooden boxes, he would have gotten out of bed and strapped on a gun.

'Of all the dirty, stinkin' lowdown varmints!' he raged. 'Kilt that young kid to hide their identity.'

'You were also a target,' Jared reminded him.

'Yeah, but at least I was responsible for getting rid of them two. Lowest durn skunks you ever set eyes on; knew they was trouble.' He heaved a sigh. 'But even then I didn't think they'd do something like this. What happened?' he asked no one in particular. 'Did God forget to give some people a conscience? Or were those two mongrels raised by a pack of coyotes?'

'I didn't get a look at the ground for several days, up where the attack took place,' Jared cut in on his tirade. 'Do you think there's any way those two could have been in this alone?'

Dodge snorted, 'About the same as me sprouting a set of wings.'

'You came pretty close, pard,' Reb put in his first comment. 'About got yourself a set of them there angel wings.'

The recovering ramrod grinned. 'Guess the good Lord didn't want me yet. Probably figured I'd raise all kinds of hell Upstairs until them killers paid their due.'

Back on track, Jared tried the same question. 'So you don't believe those two could have acted alone as far as the ambush goes?'

'Rex took a hankering to kill a rattler the second day I was on the job. Durn fool emptied his gun and never even hit it. As for Dekay, the guy didn't pack iron or a rifle.' He shook his head. 'Likewise, there were no less than four guns that opened up on us. Lonnie was betwixt me and the shooters — took the bulk of their volley. But I felt the breeze of two slugs besides the one that hit me.' He sobered and added: 'Shot my favorite horse too. Trusty steed give her life to get me back to the ranch.'

'If not for that mare's sacrifice, you'd have died for sure,' Reb declared.

'Had to be more than the two of them,' Shane returned to the original query. 'Fifty head of cattle would be quite an undertaking for two men. And, although we never saw the riders, we did find tracks of four or five horses driving the herd.'

'Surprised to see you, sonny,' Dodge spoke to Shane. 'I figured you would be traveling about putting on shows, after the success you and that . . . uh, unusual-looking mare had in Brimstone.'

'She's kind of like you and Reb,' Jared snickered. 'Getting too old for gallivanting all over creation. Come sunset, she heads for the barn.'

Dodge frowned at Reb. 'It's like I always told you, Locke should have taken a strap to Jerry more often. He's got a mouth that gets him in more trouble than a fly in a spider web.'

'Speaking of webs, we've got to put a plan in motion,' Jared turned serious. 'We are going to need a little luck to prove anything against the rustlers, slaughterhouse and tannery.'

'But you suspect you know who all is behind this rustling ring?' Dodge asked Jared.

'Since the Cattleman's Association began demanding closer inspections of brands, every major slaughterhouse has to keep records of the beef they process, including the brand of each steer.'

'According to the city editor, there has been five hundred head reported stolen in the past eighteen months on the eastern slope of Colorado alone. That's a whole lot of beef,' Shane added.

'Sic the law on them!' Dodge declared. 'Put them — what-you-call-it — collaborators? Sic the law on them and either hang 'em or put them all behind bars.'

'We're working on it,' Jared assured him. 'That's what the plan is all about. We are going to set a little trap and see if the rats take the bait.'

'Bah!' Dodge snorted. 'Was a time when we'd have taken the rustlers and everyone else involved out and strung them up from the nearest tree.'

'Just one of the many drawbacks to civilization,' Jared said. 'Nowadays, you have to have proof, a trial, get past double-talking lawyers, and a jury that isn't wearing blinders to get a conviction. Even then, they don't hang most of them.'

'Them fellers kilt young Lonnie,' Dodge reminded them. 'And you can bet he wasn't the only one that gang has dry-gulched over their past years of thieving.'

'We've got a local lawman looking into any rustling deaths, but it's going to take a little luck to bring these guys before a judge,' Jared admitted.

'I'd hate to think those sidewinders can keep getting away with their crimes.'

'We did get Rex and Dekay,' Shane reminded him. 'They were likely responsible for the theft of your cattle and for you and Lonnie getting shot. They discovered Jerry and me were on their trail and tried to put us in a grave.'

Dodge relaxed and closed his eyes. 'I reckon I can take comfort you boys got that pair.'

'We ain't giving up on the gang, pard,' Reb told him firmly. 'Like Jared says, we've got a plan.'

'Wish I could get out of bed and lend a hand, pal o' mine. Afraid age has done slowed down my healing process.'

'You keep on being yourself, making the doctors and nurses miserable,' Reb joked. 'They will shore 'nuff have you back at the ranch in another few days.'

Dodge didn't reply, having drifted off to sleep.

The boys and Reb left the room. Once outside the hospital, Reb looked skyward. 'Days are getting shorter. We need to tie this critter down and get to branding before the first snow of winter.'

Jared nodded in agreement. 'July and Wendy made their last call yesterday. They will take the train tomorrow as if leaving Denver. I spotted a guy keeping watch on the hotel on our way here. I'm guessing Pegg and Mantee are losing sleep these last few days.'

'They were watching us too,' Shane said. 'Good thing July was on alert, else we'd have been coyote fodder by now.'

'Yes, but we saw how much good he is in a fight,' Jared pointed out. 'He'd make a good target for the other side to shoot at, but I'm betting Wendy would have something to say about that.'

'She does seem sweet on him,' Shane grinned.

'No kiddin'?' Reb chuckled. 'Been wondering when she'd get bitten by the love bug.'

'I kind of thought she would look for a guy like me,' Jared said, displaying a nonplussed frown. 'After all, I'm her favorite brother.'

'Girl can't pick her relatives, but she can pick her own suitor,' Reb tossed out a jab.

'I'd take offense,' Jared reparteed, 'but neither you nor Dodge ever found a woman of your own. That is like making the rules of a game you never learned how to play.'

'Where to?' Shane wanted to know, putting an end to the banter.

Jared answered. 'As McEnroe is Fielding's supervisor, we'll lay out our plan for him. Be a good idea to have the law involved.'

'Yeah,' Reb piped up. 'Be a real shame if you two were shot by the watchman at the slaughterhouse. That would leave it up to me to get justice for Dodge and the kid.'

'Not that you couldn't handle it, but Shane and I still have some living to do.'

Jared grinned. 'He might even visit one of those places on Market Street.'

'There's some ladies over thataway who could make a man out of him.' Reb chuckled. 'Send him home strutting like a rooster.'

'Hot dang!' Shane snapped at the pair. 'I never thought I'd be saying this, but I sure wish Cliff had come along. I hate being the target of all the hazing.'

The three of them laughed together and started off down the street.

10

There had been no news since the two pests from the governor's office had visited. The last of the three days Pegg had given his crew off had passed quietly. The normal work for Saturday was scheduled to begin when Mantee showed up. It was barely light and most of the crew had not yet arrived.

'Went by your place and your pa told me you had left early.'

'Ma had a bad night,' Pegg said. 'Her condition is worse whenever the weather is warm. Don't bother her as much in the colder months.'

'That's the change-of-life thing you told me about before?'

'Yeah, raises havoc with the body temperature. Half the time it's like she is running a fever, complete with aches and pains, plus it messes with her moods and such. Good thing my pa is a saint.' He grunted. 'One more reason I'll never marry — I want someone to take care of me, not the other way around.'

Mantee chuckled. 'Are you saying you might move out of the house and get a place of your own one day soon?'

'I've got the money,' Pegg said. 'Of course, I'd have to find a good cook and housekeeper. I hate cooking or cleaning up after myself.'

'You ought to find two housekeepers while you're at it. Me and the boys could stand to have one of them around. It's a long ride into town just to get an eatable meal.'

'First, I'll likely have to get one for my folks . . . leastwise if Ma don't get past this ailment.'

'You do owe the old man. You told me your pa showed you everything you know about running this business.'

'When he started out, his work place was not much bigger than that shanty of yours,' Pegg informed him. 'Worked from daylight till dark six days every week, butchering beef, hogs, venison, and anything else the people brung in.

I remember we plucked chickens, ducks and turkeys, along with dressing out rabbits, goats — you name it. I was sixteen by the time he had enough business to start up this place, an actual slaughterhouse.'

Mantee snorted. 'My folks kicked me out when I was sixteen. It was either that or turn me over to the law.' He shrugged. 'I ran with a wild pack back then.'

Pegg grunted. 'Then you decided to start a pack of your own.'

'Near twenty years on my own and never spent more than a night in jail for drinking or brawling. Never held a real job in my life.' He harrumphed. 'Of course, trying to make that ranch look respectable has got me a handful of blisters and an aching back. When I joined up with you, I never wanted to settle down and actually work cattle!'

'Soon as those pesky government people are done, we'll butcher or sell the cattle on the ranch and you and me can both get back to business.'

'That's why I'm here early,' Mantee

told him. 'Rocco followed the pair — the guy and girl who were doing the survey or whatever it was — and I wanted you to know what was going on.'

'And?' Pegg prompted him to continue.

'They made a trip out to see your meat-cutter yesterday, then they went to the governor's office. After that, they bought train tickets for tomorrow morning.'

'Train tickets? Do you know where they are going?'

'Heading back to Cheyenne. Guess that's where they come from. Pitkin probably didn't trust anyone local to gather the information. Could have figured they might have been bought off or something. Anyway, they are gone.'

'Yes, but what . . . '

Pegg stopped speaking as a door closed down the hall. Before he could move over to look and see who it was, Don Larson entered his office. He stopped, seeing Mantee.

'Oh,' he excused his interruption. 'I didn't think you would have anyone here so early.'

'What is it, Don?'

'Just something I wanted to speak to you about. It can wait.'

'Actually,' Mantee broke in quickly. 'I was on my way to town. I'll stop back on my return trip and we can discuss when you might need some more beef.'

'That's fine,' Pegg was agreeable, gesturing to Don. 'Come inside and sit down.'

Don couldn't help feeling nervous as he sat down on a wooden chair, but this was something he had to do. He waited until Pegg closed the door and took his place behind the desk. When the man folded his hands on the desktop, he began.

'I don't know if this is important or not, but I thought you ought to know.'

'Go ahead,' Pegg encouraged.

'Well, a couple of people came to visit me at my house during my days off. They said they were from the governor's office — showed me an official-looking paper.'

'Yes, they stopped by here as well. It's a survey that has something to do with future growth and new businesses coming to Denver.'

'Told me the same thing,' Don said. 'But they began questioning me about cattle brands and if I had seen this one or that.' He hurried to add, 'Of course I told them I didn't pay much attention to the holding pens around back. I enter by the side door and the rear of the building is for . . . well, for Everett to do his thing. I don't mind cutting meat, but I've never been able to stand the smell out back.'

'Yes, Ingram claims to have lost his sense of smell during the war. I'm certain it helps him to deal with the rendering process.'

'Anyway, they kept trying to pin me down to the number of beef for these past coupla weeks. I told them we'd been busy, but I didn't have any way to keep count. I filled the orders you gave me and that was it.'

'That's fine,' his boss assured him. 'Telling the truth is always best.'

'The two let something else slip, something I thought you might want to know.'

'And what's that?'

Don leaned forward as if uncomfortable and kept his voice down. 'They said they had talked to a couple range detectives, two guys who were trying to track down some cattle rustlers. They warned me that those investigators might show up here.'

Pegg's eyes grew a bit colder but he waved a hand to dismiss the story. 'If they do, there's nothing to find. We have a record of all of the cattle sold and processed here. They will be wasting their time.'

Don relaxed in the chair. 'Whew! I'm glad to get that out of the way. I know we deal with the Big M ranch for a good many of our beef, and Everett once told me those guys do a lot of buying and selling. I was afraid some of those cattle might not have the proper brands or paperwork.'

'No, every beef we take in has the brand recorded. I verify every purchase personally.'

Don rose to his feet. 'Good enough. I just thought you ought to know.'

'And I thank you for coming forward. I'll make sure all of my paperwork is in order, so it will be ready for inspection if those investigators show up.'

Don started for the door and stopped. 'Oh, I wanted to thank you for the three days off and the twenty-five-dollar bonus. The wife spent most of it on the kids, but we had a nice three days.'

'You earned every bit of it,' Pegg replied. 'I appreciate the hard work you do.'

Don went on out, heading for the change room to put on his work clothes and apron. It was a little early to start work, but he had done what he had come to do.

* * *

It was late when Mantee made the return trip and stopped at the slaughterhouse. He found a very anxious and pacing Singeon Pegg waiting for him.

'The storm is heading our way,' Pegg wasted no time telling him what was going on. 'I got a tip this afternoon. There's going to be a raid on this place tomorrow. Being Sunday, those two range detectives are gonna come here and go through all of my files and records. They intend to get some kind of order from the governor or judge to check my bank account too.'

'Damn!' Mantee exclaimed, whirling about for the door. 'We best pack our gear and git.'

Pegg shot out a hand and caught hold of his arm. 'Hold it!' he barked the order. 'We aren't gonna run from them two snoops.'

'But they will put us all behind bars!'

Pegg snorted his disdain. 'We are not going anywhere!' Then swearing vehemently, he vowed, 'But those two interfering Valerons are. In fact, they are going to disappear from the face of the earth.'

'How?' Mantee cried, his brow suddenly beaded with the sweat of fear. 'Tell me how!'

'First, are Kidd and his pals still out at your place?'

'I done like you said — they ain't showed their faces in Denver.'

Pegg walked over and sat down behind his desk. As Mantee was no longer ready to bolt from the room, he took a chair and waited for the boss to sort out his plan. Pegg mulled a few ideas over before he finally began to speak.

'Who is the most intimidating and ruthless man working for us?'

'Intim . . . a what?'

'The meanest-looking critter on the payroll. Preferably not real well recognized around these parts.'

'Was I walking down a dark alleyway at night, that there Victor is a man I wouldn't want to meet. He looks like he'd eat a live snake and give the snake first bite.'

'Victor? One of Kidd's men?'

'Dixon brought along him and a Frenchman name Ponce. They both have been dodging posses and wanted posters for the past few years. They latched onto

Kidd when he got out of prison, 'cause Dix don't usually get caught.'

'I want Victor to throw a scare into someone, while we are dealing with the Valerons.'

'Right.'

'As for the rest of you, I've thought up a way to get rid of those two and put us in the clear. When we finish with the Valerons, there won't be a shred of evidence against us . . . and not a trace that those two ever existed.'

'Tell me what you want and I'll get it done.'

Pegg gave a bob of his head, satisfied that this was the only way. He had never involved himself in murder, but this was his life. He had worked and slaved for years, finally to reach a degree of success. A couple of nosy cowboys weren't going to ruin everything now.

* * *

Sunday morning arrived, along with the train going north. It had one more stop before crossing the empty expanse between Denver and Cheyenne. July and Wendy were certain they had been seen, so they were doing their part of the plan by leaving.

'Are you ready to return to the boring daily grind of punching cattle?' Wendy asked, after a few minutes of travel.

'It's interesting work, but I liked using my head and helping with adding up those figures and such. I always was good at doing my numbers. When it came to mining, T L let me handle all of the deciphering the worth of our ore from each ton we mined and everything to do with money or figures.'

'Martin has taught me enough to assume the bookkeeping and accounting for some of the businesses in Valeron. His work load is simply too much, so I'm going to help.'

'Sounds like a good job. You sure seem to know your bookkeeping and such.'

Wendy enjoyed the way July never questioned her ability or statements. A good many men would have guffawed at the thought of a woman managing the accounting end of one or more businesses on her own. But he accepted she could do whatever she claimed and was actually supportive.

'With so much work — the handling of three or four of our stores — I would likely need to hire a bookkeeper to help.' She took a deep breath, summoning her courage. 'Would you be interested in that kind of work?'

'You mean, sitting in a warm office in the cold of winter, making entries in a journal or ledger, then tallying the numbers and checking totals against inventory and the like?'

'That's about it.' She lifted a careless shoulder in a shrug. 'Of course, you would not be out in the fresh air, riding a horse, tending cattle, branding, feeding, mending fences, pulling night watch during bad weather or the like. Perhaps you would miss it.'

His winsome grin brightened his face. 'If the job allowed me to work alongside you, I'd help with the laundry or cooking chores.'

Wendy laughed. 'You do know there would be actual work involved — book-keeping is tedious and causes eyestrain and headaches.'

'Moving a herd is a lot of dust, wind and sun too — hard on the whole body.'

'After this adventure is behind us, I'll speak to Father and Martin. I'll let them know we are . . . um, compatible.'

'Compatible,' he repeated. 'That sounds like a word I could take to heart.'

'You know its meaning?'

'Reckon I've heard it used enough to know it has more than one meaning. Might get a man like me to thinking he has a shot at courting the most sought-after gal in the country.'

Wendy felt a tingle race along her spine while her heart beat faster. 'After saving Jared and Shane from being murdered in cold blood, you have earned the gratitude of me and my father. I'd say that gives you a big step up on courting.'

'I sure wouldn't want you allowing me the privilege just because of that . . . my being at the right place at the right time.'

'Don't sell yourself short,' she replied. 'You have a lot to offer a girl.'

'I only have myself and all that I'll ever have or be, Miss Wendy. But I'd sure enough give it all to you.'

Wendy didn't have an answer to that. She knew it would take only the slightest encouragement and they would wind up in an embrace. Choosing to let the subject lie, rather than possibly ending up being kissed in public, she gave a slight nod of her head and looked out the window at the passing scenery.

'I don't know,' July spoke up after a few tense moments. 'This seems a good plan, but I'm a little worried about the Larson family.'

Wendy looked back at him with a perplexed expression. From a declaration of affection to mentioning a meatcutter's personal safety? She gulped her romantic reverie down like swallowing too big of a bite of food and squeaked out, 'What are you talking about?'

'Suppose Pegg gets to thinking about

good old *Honest* Don Larson? What if he decides Larson is a risk? I mean, this crook is looking at a rope or a good many years in prison. If he thinks Larson might go to the law or testify in court against him . . . '

He didn't have to finish the statement. Wendy leapt on board with his notion. 'We didn't allow any contingency for that.'

'I don't know that word, but I reckon you know what I'm talking about.'

Wendy sat up straight and looked out the window.

'We're almost to the last stop before the open country. Grab our things; we're getting off the train!'

* * *

Jared and Shane discovered Officer Fielding was not available, having been dispatched to look into a farmer's complaint about a wild animal killing their chickens. Sergeant McEnroe volunteered to help with their plan and had already spoken to the judge on their behalf. He was there to meet them at the livery after breakfast.

'You think we might have trouble?' Jared asked the lawman.

'Shouldn't be any problem,' McEnroe replied. 'Being Sunday, Pegg will only have his usual watchman at the slaughter-house. He is a crippled ex-Union soldier that I've known for some time. He spends more time sleeping than patrolling the grounds. He won't give us any trouble.' He put a hand up to his uniform and patted the pocket. 'Besides, I've got the order from the judge right here. It states we have the right to remove all of the pertinent records for evidence.'

'I'm glad the judge took our word about what we suspected,' Jared said.

'Turns out, the governor just completed an audit of the local businesses — done by a couple of out-of-town accountants — and they mentioned there were some irregularities concerning Pegg's bookkeeping. On paper the man has purchased just over a hundred cattle this year, yet his production and sales show enough beef to more than double that.'

'An audit you say. Are you talking about July Colby?' Jared displayed innocence. 'He said his job was something concerning the governor.'

'Yes. He and a young lady collected the data and wrote up a report. I was the one responsible for checking their findings and then forwarding the document to the governor's desk.'

Shane chipped in, 'And that's what allowed you to get the warrant from the judge so we could confiscate Pegg's records?'

'Exactly.'

Shane followed his reply with another query. 'Then once we prove Pegg has been butchering stolen cattle, you will arrest him?'

'Him and anyone tied to the rustling ring,' McEnroe assured them. 'We looked into it and there have been six other men shot or injured during raids to steal cattle this past year. Two of them were killed, which makes three with the young fellow from the Barrett ranch. Dodge was very fortunate.'

Jared rubbed his chin. 'With them being guilty of several murders, they will likely put up a fight. I wonder if you ought to bring along a couple of men, in case we run into the rustlers.'

'The tannery and slaughterhouse are both shut down tight on Sundays,' McEnroe responded. 'We won't have any trouble today.'

'And once we get the books?' Shane asked.

'The captain will provide me with the needed men the minute the judge issues the warrants.' He waved a careless hand. 'Trust me, boys, if those records pan out, we'll have every guilty man-jack of them behind bars by tomorrow night.'

'Let's hit the saddles,' Jared was eager to get started. 'The sooner them fellows are behind bars, the sooner we can head for home.'

* * *

July and Wendy picked up a couple horses at a small stable and hurried back along the main trail. They went by the livery when they arrived in town, only to learn Jared and Shane had left an hour earlier.

'Maybe we ought to get one of the lawmen to ride with us?' July offered, as they mounted up again.

Wendy shook her head. 'We don't know for certain anything will happen. You and I ought to be able to handle whatever comes up. There's a good chance no one will even trouble the Larsons.'

'Just remember, I don't shoot for shucks, Miss Wendy.'

They started off and kept a steady pace. Wendy turned to July and said: 'I'm sure the Larson family attends a Sunday meeting — probably fairly close by. I doubt they would bring their kids all the way into the city.'

'Yeah, come winter, that would be a real chore.'

'So we should have plenty of time.'

After a short way, July again let his

worry show through. 'Supposing Jared and Shane can't prove anything with Pegg's records?'

Wendy grinned. 'My brother knows how to get a confession out of a guilty party.'

'Did he tell you the whole plan? I mean, there has to be more to it than using the daily orders and accounting records. How can they prove anything against the Big M ranch? And what if the tannery is involved?'

'Do you have faith in me?'

July blinked in surprise at the question. 'Boy, howdy! I don't reckon I ever met anyone I have more faith in than you — and that includes T L.'

'Well, I have complete faith in Jerry. I can't remember a time when he ever set out to do a job and it didn't get done. Plus, he's been there for me a time or two before. And I mean, really been there.'

'I recollect the story your foreman feller, Sketcher, told me about him and the others going after your kidnapped sister. That's about the wildest tale I ever heard — especially as it's all true.'

'And you saw the cutout from the Denver newspaper about him and Wyatt bringing in those killers with ropes strung between the outlaw's horses.'

'Yep, neck-to-neck-to-neck prisoners,' he recalled. 'I'd never seen or heard of anything to beat that either.'

'Well, if you stick around long enough, you'll learn that most everyone in our family can be counted on when needed . . . and they will do whatever is necessary to complete their task.'

July grinned. 'Like I said, we don't have to worry about your brother. Let's figure a way to do our little chore without messing it up.'

Wendy laughed. 'Now you are sounding more like the man I . . . ' She paused, a flush of color rushing to her cheeks.

'The man you what?' July asked, taking notice of her odd expression.

'I . . . ' she shrugged her shoulders. 'I almost said something inappropriate.'

'You?' he was shocked. 'But you never misuse a word. I don't know that . . . '

But this time, he stopped speaking.

After a short way and a much longer silence, July cast a sidelong glace at Wendy. 'You didn't about say the word . . . *love*, did you?'

Wendy squirmed, finding the saddle suddenly hard and uncomfortable. 'It was a slip — well, it would have been a slip of the tongue.' She made eye contact, but with a coy, somewhat defensive look. 'It's just that I've grown used to you, and the only other men I am at ease with are related to me. Or like Reb and Dodge — longtime friends. I've often told them something like: *it's why I love you*.'

'I'm truly pleased to think you consider me as one of those close friends,' July said carefully. 'Even,' he hurried to add, 'if it was a slip.'

'Is that what we are, July?' Wendy asked gently. 'Are we close friends?'

July licked his lips, as if he had suddenly lost the moisture to form words. 'Uh, well, to be completely honest with you, I'd sure like to be a whole lot more.'

Wendy smiled. 'Me too.'

The man sat up straight in the saddle. 'Then let's get this here chore taken care of, Miss Wendy. I'm for the two of us going to a dance or some other social affair. Nothing I'd like more than to have you on my arm.'

'It's a date,' she replied. 'Soon as we put this chore behind us.'

11

Everything looked quiet at the slaughterhouse. One horse was tethered at the holding corral, able to eat from a manger used whenever cattle were penned inside. From the office window, a man was visible sitting in a chair by the window. His hat was tipped down over his eyes and he appeared to be asleep.

'See what I told you?' McEnroe said in a hushed voice. 'Old Barney never was much of a watchman.'

'We'll let you talk to him,' Jared suggested. 'Don't want to spook the old guy and give him apoplexy.'

The three tied off their horses at the hitch-rail and went up to the front door of the building. It wasn't locked so they walked into the main office.

'Yo there, Barney!' McEnroe spoke loudly. 'You asleep, old timer?'

The man in the chair lifted his head. Once unveiled from the floppy hat, they saw it was not the old watchman — it was Pegg! Before Jared could react a gun was shoved against his ribs. Into the room spilled four more men, all with guns drawn.

Jared looked down to see the gun pressed to his side was held by the police sergeant. He and Shane had no chance. They were both quickly disarmed and their hands were tied behind their backs.

'Should have known a rustling operation like this would have someone spying from the local law,' he grated between his teeth at McEnroe. 'You're as guilty of murder and thieving as any of these others.'

'Unlike the rest of those dummies working for the police, I don't intend to risk my neck for pennies and die broke,' McEnroe told him.

'Good work, Mac,' Pegg praised his accomplice. 'Neatly done.'

Of the others, one was Mantee and another looked vaguely familiar.

'You remind me of a man I arrested some time back,' Jared spoke to him.

'You related to one of those three me and my cousin brought to justice?'

'Brought him to be lynched, you mean!' The man snarled. 'Timmy was my brother.'

'Dixon Kidd,' Jared pinned a name on him. 'I saw you had been released from prison a few months back.'

'I'm here to even the score, Valeron,' Dixon sneered the words. 'We're gonna gut you like one of the beef, melt the flesh off of your bones, then grind your left-over bones to meal. No one is ever going to know what happened to you and your kin here.'

'Dad gum! When you fix to get even, you don't mess around,' Jared replied.

Pegg looked at Mantee. 'You keeping watch? We don't want anyone passing by to see something they shouldn't.'

'Rocco is outside.' Mantee tipped his head to another man. 'Jones, you go keep an eye out with him. Get the horses from the draw. Soon as we deal with these two, we'll wrap their bodies in canvas and tote them over to the tannery.'

'That's how you intend to melt our flesh,' Jared surmised. 'Toss our bodies into a vat of lime or whatever, then grind the bones and there will be no trace left.'

'Plus, we will burn everything you own, including your clothes and saddles. Your horses will have to be done away with too.' Pegg shrugged. 'Fortunately, I own this here butchering house. Won't be anything left of them for anyone to ever find either.'

'And the story about where we went?'

'Far as we know,' McEnroe interjected, 'you two boys left to follow the trail of them stolen beef. Something must have happened to you between here and Pueblo. That's a long way — close to a hundred miles. Who knows how you met your fate?'

'You forget the findings of those two auditors for the governor. It's going to look real suspicious having us disappear after they gave him their findings.'

McEnroe burst forth with a menacing laugh. 'I was the one who checked over the findings,' he said. 'It didn't take but a few changes and everything looks perfectly innocent. There was no discrepancy between buying and selling of Pegg's beef in the paper I forwarded to the governor.'

'You had us nailed from the very start,' Jared allowed them a victory. 'I have to admit, this is the smartest rustling ring I ever heard of — the slaughterhouse, the law, all the way down to the tannery. Makes an honest man believe he's working at a real disadvantage.'

'Enough jawboning,' Dixon growled. 'Let's herd this pair into the back and dress 'em out like we would a mountain buck. I've a mind to hear these two scream like a couple of frightened little girls!'

McEnroe shook his head. 'I'm not a part of this. You keep paying me and I'll keep providing information, but I draw the line at murder.'

'So git, law-dog!' Dixon barked at him. 'You done your part.'

McEnroe hurried out of the office to get his horse. He wanted to be miles away before Dixon Kidd took his revenge on the Valerons.

'Scooted away like a kid what just turned over an outhouse!' Dixon laughed to Pegg. 'Let's get started.'

'Soon as Rocco gives us the all-clear,' Pegg ordered. 'He'll check the trail both ways to make sure we're not interrupted. Soon as he gives the go-ahead, the Valerons are at your mercy.'

Dixon guffawed, 'Yeah, like they are getting any of that from me!'

* * *

Don was in the process of putting the carryall away, having just unharnessed his horse, when the two men appeared from inside his small barn. Thankfully, Gayle had taken the children into the house to change from their Sunday best to everyday clothes.

'You waiting for me, fellers?' he asked.

The men were both strangers — one a medium-framed man with a mustache, and the other a rough-looking brute with savage eyes and a scar on one cheek.

'Nice family you have, Larson,' Brute said.

'Ez true, *monsieur*,' the other spoke in a distinct French accent. 'You must be very proud.'

'My wife and children are all I live for,' Don replied carefully. 'Can I help you with something?'

The two closed the distance until they had Don blocked between them. He saw menace in their faces, but he had no weapon at hand.

Brute looked him up and down, as one might appraise a horse. 'Pretty little woman, your wife,' he said. 'Be a real shame if she had to raise them kids on her own.'

'What are you talking about?'

'Have no fear, *monsieur*,' Frenchy said, his voice calm, yet menacing. 'We wish you no harm.'

'Then why . . .'

'The thing is,' Brute cut him off, 'if a man was to run off at the mouth. . . . Well, that could be very unhealthy. Your wife could end up a widow real quick.'

'I don't know what . . . '

Frenchy raised a hand to stop his protest. 'We think you do.'

Brute's hand shot out and he took hold of Don's throat. He squeezed hard enough that Don gagged and put both of his own hands around the man's wrists, trying to break the hold.

'It's real simple,' Brute threatened, throttling him. 'You even think of talking to the law or anyone else about what you might have seen — or thought you saw — at the slaughterhouse, and we'll be back.'

'Listen to my friend,' Frenchy warned. 'Yours ez not the only life you have to worry about. There ez your wife, your children . . . Be smart, *monsieur*. Do as we say!'

'I think you'd best do what *we* say!' July voiced the command from behind them.

Brute released Don and both henchmen rotated about to see July and Wendy about thirty feet away — he with a handgun pointed at them and she with a rifle in her hands.

Brute pushed Don hard enough that he lost his footing and sat down. He raked the newcomers with malevolent eyes. Then a snarl curled his lips.

'You're shaking like a leaf in a high wind, little man,' he directed his attention to July. 'I don't think you ever pointed a gun at a man before.' With a grunt, 'Especially one who could rip your head right off of your shoulders!'

'Oui, monsieur,' Frenchy joined him, one hand on the butt of his gun. 'I think we can kill you before you have time to act.'

Wendy cocked her rifle and threw it to her shoulder. With the weapon aligned at either of the pair, she was next to speak.

'I'm a Valeron,' she stated succinctly. 'My brothers taught me to shoot when I was ten years old, and I'm as good with this rifle as anyone in my family. Both of you toss your guns away or we will kill you.'

Frenchy lifted his hands, but Brute took a threatening step in her direction.

Wendy pulled the trigger.

Brute howled in surprise and lifted a hand to find a piece of his ear was missing. Before he had time to recover Wendy cocked the rifle and had it ready again.

'If you'd like further proof I *can* and *will* kill you, tough guy,' Wendy warned a second time, 'take one more step!'

July cocked the hammer back on his handgun. 'I might be shaking some, but I'm not afraid to use this gun either. You best do as Miss Valeron tells you.'

Frenchy used two fingers to remove his gun, then flipped it aside. Brute was still fingering his bleeding ear with one hand, but used the other to discard his weapon.

'Mr Larson,' July took charge. 'We'd be obliged if you would round up some twine or rope and tie the hands of these men behind their backs. We'll be taking them to jail in town.'

'I'll saddle my horse and go with you. I see Gayle is standing in the doorway. She certainly heard the gunshot and must be going crazy wondering what is going on.'

'Tie them up first, then explain things to your wife,' July recommended. 'Me and Miss Valeron will get them on their horses and make sure they are secure for the trip into Denver.'

As Don began to bind the hands of the two intruders, Wendy smiled at July. 'You handled that pretty well.'

'I about left my boots when you pulled the trigger. It's lucky for them I didn't start shooting before I knew what was going on.'

She laughed. 'Actually, I was just showing off. Jerry always said I was as good as him — I wanted to prove him right.'

'Any idea who these two men are?'

'If they were here to warn Mr Larson to keep quiet, they are working with Pegg. We'll have them put behind bars while we wait for Jer and Shane.'

'How do you think they are doing?'

'Should be tying up loose ends of their own by now,' Wendy said confidently.

* * *

With ropes around their wrists, both Shane and Jared were dangling from meat hooks, the ones used after the beef were skinned. As the two men were nearly the same height, their toes just touched the floor so they could relieve some of the strain on their wrists.

'What's taking so long?' Dixon demanded to know. 'I'm ready to start carving!'

Pegg held up a hand to prevent him from doing anything. 'Let me see what's holding Rocco up. He should have checked the area by now.'

Mantee shook his head at Dixon. 'You sure you want to do it like this? I mean, to kill a man is one thing, but butchering him like a hog — while he's still conscious?'

'If you ain't got the stomach, get the hell out.'

Mantee looked at Squint. 'Let's join Rocco and Jones outside. I don't hate anyone enough to watch them being skinned alive.'

'This place smells to high heaven too,' Squint returned. 'You can see the floor is slanted so the blood runs to that gutter and drains outside, but . . . damn! I don't know how a man stands the stench day after day.'

'Ought to stick your nose into the rendering room,' Mantee told him. 'You'd never enjoy the taste of steak again.'

Then Squint and Mantee turned toward the side door, following after Pegg.

Dixon ripped Jared's shirt off and snickered. 'Any last words — before you start screaming your lungs out?'

Jared clenched his teeth together and hissed: 'Yeah . . you're all under arrest!'

Pegg didn't reach the side door, but stopped dead in his tracks. He backed up right into Mantee and Squint — with his hands raised.

'No one move!' Locke Valeron's booming voice commanded.

Wyatt Valeron, along with Reb, charged into the room.

Dixon didn't think — he reacted —

trying to draw his gun.

A bullet from Wyatt's Colt staggered him. He had managed to get his own weapon clear and desperately tried to point it at Jared. . . .

Another gun blast filled the closed-in room.

Dixon pitched forward and his face bounced off the bloodstained floor. Unable to raise himself up, he turned his head and glared at Jared until the vacancy of death filled his eyes.

Squint, Mantee and Pegg were quickly stripped of weapons and bound up for travel. Locke himself used a knife to cut down his son and nephew.

'You took your sweet time, Pa,' Jared complained. 'If Pegg hadn't been concerned with anyone happening by to hear our cries, Shane and I would be *half the men* we were when this thing started.'

'And he does mean half the men,' Shane repeated. 'I've never been so scared in my life.'

'*Hanging* around with Jared . . . 'Wyatt snickered at the pun, 'will do that to you, cousin.'

Jared harrumphed. 'I'll laugh about this some day, but this isn't that day. I'm for thinking my soul left my body about ten minutes ago — couldn't stand the notion of how much suffering we expected.'

'The two men watching outside were tough to take out silently,' Locke informed the pair. 'Takoda and Chayton might have been the pride of the army scouts back in their day, but they work a whole lot slower than in their youth.'

Officer Fielding entered the room, having come in from the office. 'I found the journals we need. He looked at the body on the floor and shook his head. 'There wasn't to be any killing.'

'Didn't have a choice,' Wyatt explained. 'Locke told everyone not to move.'

'You can see Dixon's gun is out,' Jared directed his attention to the dead man's weapon. 'He wanted to take me with him.'

'Had I give it some thought, I might have let him shoot first,' Wyatt snickered.

'Jerry has been a thorn in the family's side for a good many years.'

'Who has shot more men than me and any other two Valerons?' Jared fired back. 'That would be you!'

'Did you nab McEnroe?' Locke remained focused to the job.

'Cliff was watching the road at that end — no way the back-stabbing lawman could have gotten past him. Him and your Indian wranglers will have McEnroe and the two guards ready for travel.'

Jared took a mental count. 'Wait a minute. Dixon wouldn't have been alone, and we have Mantee and his four men.'

'Maybe they are over at the tannery,' Shane postulated. 'You can bet someone is waiting to finish the job on us.'

'Tannery? What are you talking about, nephew?' Locke asked him.

'They were going to stick our bodies in a vat of brine or whatever bath they use to remove the extra meat and hair off of the cowhides. After that, our bones would be ground to meal and ka'flooie! — we do a disappearing act like at one of those carnival magician's shows.'

'Ka'flooie, huh?' Locke said, displaying a frown. 'I'm glad you killed Dixon, Wyatt,' Locke told him. 'I've suddenly developed a major dislike of the man.'

'How about it, Pegg?' Reb pulled his skinning knife. 'Where are Dixon's missing men?'

'They had orders not to hurt anyone,' Pegg said quickly. 'Two of them rode over to warn my meat-cutter not to say anything. That's all I know about them.'

'Jared,' Locke ordered, 'you and Wyatt take a ride over there. We'll meet you at the jail in town.'

'What about the tannery?'

'We'll stop by and pick up whoever is waiting to help dispose of your body.'

Wyatt snickered. 'Tell them Jared can generally use a cleaning, but he isn't real keen on taking a dip in anything quite so harsh as lime.'

* * *

Don Larson stood before Bingham Pegg with his hat in his hands and a lowered head. He had helped take the two hired goons into town with Wendy and July. He'd been there when Officer Fielding and the Valerons showed up with all of their prisoners in tow. He informed the man about his son and the crimes they would be answering to.

'You mean Hank Grubber was part of a rustling operation?' Bingham did not hide his incredulity. 'I thought him an honest man.'

'And the police sergeant, McEnroe, was involved too.'

Bingham heaved a sigh. 'I knew some chicanery must be going on, Don. I mean, my boy was making more money than I ever imagined running that place. I couldn't figure out how he could manage it, unless he was doing something underhanded.'

'The Big M ranch is in your name, Mr Pegg. The Valerons showed me the paperwork. As for the rest of it, I know a little about buying and selling beef.

It didn't take a lot of looking to see the books had been fixed. The discrepancy between the amount of beef purchased and the amount sold — it was impossible to cover up.'

The elderly man was despondent. 'My son, a crook and a would-be murderer.'

'When the court had the bank records checked, your son has more than twenty thousand dollars in his account.'

'Mantee, Grubber, McEnroe . . . it's sad what greed can do.'

'I'm real sorry, Mr Pegg,' Don told him. 'I guess your boy wanted to be wealthy and took the shortest route to reach his goal.'

'What is to be done about the slaughterhouse?'

'It has to stay open,' Don said. 'The entire valley depends on it for meat — and same for the tannery. Hank said his brother would come up from Santa Fe to assume control of it. Hank expects to get a couple years behind bars for processing hides from rustled beef. I'm not sure about your son. He claims he never ordered anyone hurt during the rustling. If the judge feels sorry for him, he might only get a few years too.'

'You said he was arrested while in the process of preparing to murder two men — those Valerons.' He uttered a conclusive grunt. 'Can't see any judge overlooking that.'

'You're probably right.'

'I'll take over the running of the slaughterhouse again,' Bingham decided. 'However, I'll want to hire another meat-cutter.'

Don felt a sinking in his stomach. 'I understand. I didn't hide what little I knew from the investigators. I probably helped them to discover the truth of the rustling ring.'

'That might be true,' Bingham countered. 'However, I'm not looking to replace you; I'm looking to promote you. When we were working together, you mentioned you ran your own business for a time. With a little of my help, you can learn to run this business for me.'

Don was speechless for a moment.

Then he gasped, 'You want me to manage the operation?'

Bingham grinned, in spite of the mental anguish he was suffering. 'Yes, son, I want you to manage it. Like I said, I'll lend a hand for a little while, but I'm too old for the daily grind. I will sell the Big M, with however many cattle there are with it and retire again, here with my wife.'

'Thank you, sir! I'll sure do the best job I know how.'

'I don't know what you were being paid, but you can put yourself down for double the amount and we'll decide on a percent of the net profit to add to that.'

'Yes, sir,' Don said. 'That's very generous!'

'Tomorrow is Monday. You need to arrive early and get a jump on the orders. I'll be there after I visit my son and find out when he is to go on trial.'

'I'll make sure everything is kept on schedule.'

Bingham reached out and shook Don's hand. 'It's a sorry way to get a promotion, but I figure you'll do me a good honest job.'

'Yes, sir, I will.'

* * *

Locke sat with Wendy on the train, while July shared a place next to Shane. Cliff and the two Indians had left for home the previous day.

'I feel that I should have stayed with Jared and Wyatt,' Wendy spoke after a time. 'After all, it was our audit that exposed the extra beef. The judge might have wanted that part of the investigation to be explained in court.'

'Officer Fielding assured me the charges were irrefutable. With the rustling, a murder charge and attempted murder of Jared and Shane — most of those men will offer up only a plea for leniency. Jared can testify if necessary, but it sounded as if the judge was a good man.'

'Yes, but I shot the one bruiser who arrived to threaten Mr Larson's family. What about my testimony for that?'

Locke chuckled. 'I think you feel a bit cheated, dear daughter. You did something quite daring and heroic and would have enjoyed a bit of the glory.'

'Daddy, you make me sound self-promoting, wanting to bathe in the light of my deeds.'

'We are all proud of you, Wendy,' Locke told her seriously. 'We've always been very proud of you.'

'So what about my idea for my new job?'

'You mean taking a green cowhand and making him a bookkeeper?'

'Trust you to make the position sound small and trivial, Father.'

Locke put a stern look on her. 'Why is it, that when you are coercing me into doing something, you call me *Dad*? Yet if I balk at your notion or don't give in right away, I become *Father*?'

Wendy looked him in square in the eye. 'You know me very well . . . Daddy,' she said carefully. 'You might as well know that I'm very fond of July Colby too.'

'Do tell?'

'We haven't done any formal courting, but it is something we intend to do. I would like your permission and support.'

'And if I don't give it?'

Without skipping a beat: 'Then I'll do it anyway.'

He laughed at her brazen honesty. 'Wendy, honey,' he said lovingly, 'you know I only want what is best for you. And I've told each and every child in our family the same thing — once you reach the age of twenty-one, your mother and I accept you as fully grown-up adults. By that time, we assume you have learned enough to make your own decisions.'

Wendy started to speak, but he held up a hand to stop her.

'However,' he continued to lecture her, 'when it comes to running the ranch or overseeing our many operations or businesses, that is not up to anyone but myself, Udal and Temple. We three brothers share the heavy responsible of taking care of all our families and all of those people who work for us. There is no room for bias or preferential treatment.'

'Yes, Father,' Wendy acquiesced. 'I understand.'

'That being said, for the job of overseeing four of our businesses, I'm happy to allow you to hire whomever you please . . . so long as they prove competent in their tasks.'

Wendy put on one of her pixie expressions. 'You have the most infuriating way of dictating terms, Daddy.'

'It's the only weapon I have against being so easily manipulated by your charms.'

'Then you approve of July?'

'Even when I don't approve of your choices, Wendy, I trust you to make the right decision.'

She stood up, forcing him to be a gentleman and rise to his feet as well. He looked puzzled over her action.

'As you trust my decisions, I'm making one.' She flashed him a playful grin. 'I'm going to trade places with Shane and sit with my young man.'

He moved into the center aisle to allow her to exit their seat. 'Fine,' he said with some relief. 'I rather enjoy conversing with Shane. I can't remember a single time he has ever caused me dyspepsia or a headache.'

* * *

Jared and Wyatt walked from the courthouse with Officer Fielding. The judge had directed a trial be held the following week. The charges ranged from murder and rustling for Mantee and his men, to attempted murder and accessory to rustling for Pegg. Dixon Kidd's two men had outstanding warrants and would be turned over to a US Marshal and transferred to the courts from whence those charges had been made. As for McEnroe, he was facing numerous offenses for having been working with Pegg, including accessory to attempted murder, and undermining the authority of the local police.

'I have to thank you Valerons,' Fielding

spoke up. 'I got promoted to McEnroe's job. My title is now Sergeant Fielding.'

'Congratulations, sergeant,' Jared said. 'It's a promotion well earned.'

'Especially,' Wyatt quipped, 'since you got to the slaughterhouse in time to save Jared's hide . . . literally.'

Fielding shook hands with both men and left to go back to work.

'I think you are right,' Wyatt told Jared, once they were alone. 'I saw Wendy and July holding hands.' He narrowed his look. 'Do you feel the guy is right for her?'

'He risked his life to save me and Shane,' Jared answered. 'Got to give him credit. That took courage.'

'A good many men would have done the same thing.'

'You haven't seen the guy hold a gun. He might as well have been unarmed. That's why I say he has courage.'

Wyatt accepted his statement. 'I suppose you know, if Wendy up and marries Colby, it will leave you as Locke's only unwed offspring.'

'We ended up with Cliff and little Nessy in our household too,' Jared replied. 'If he ever gets himself a wife, it will be because of that little girl. She's a sweetheart.'

'Makes you want to have one of your own, huh?'

'Wyatt, you and I are cut from the same bolt of cloth. We enjoy the adventure of being on our own, doing what we want, when we want, and being answerable to no one.'

'We are both looking down a very short road until we are thirty years old, Jer. Time and our way of life take a toll. One day soon, we might both decide to hang up our guns and end our traveling ways. We could take a regular job, have a wife and kids waiting for us to get home nights, go to church on Sundays and have family get-togethers with the folks once or twice a month.'

The two men stood thoughtfully for a moment . . . then looked at each other.

'Naw, that isn't me!' Jared said, grinning.

Wyatt laughed. 'Me neither!'

Then the two of them walked down the street together, trying to decide where they would have a bite to eat.

Other titles in the
Linford Western Library:

THE LORDS OF THE PLAINS

Paul Bedford

Josiah Wakefield and his friend Dan Sturgis find work as troubleshooters for the Union Pacific Railroad. The pair discover that someone is supplying Sioux warriors with repeating rifles, and that stolen 'Double Eagles' are the incentive. Recovering the gold turns out to be simple: keeping hold of it is something else entirely. Unsure who they can trust, they return to the railhead. Here, they make a stand against all comers, in the hope that they can finally bring the ringleader to account.

WHITEOUT!

Jay D. West

When the woman he loves marries someone else, Henry Mullins decides to ride off into the great unknown. Intending to get to Los Angeles, he is forced inland and eventually into the Sierra Nevadas, where he starts to trap wild animals to stay alive. Attacked by wolves, bears and the elements, Henry gradually learns the art of survival. Winter sets in high in the mountains, Henry's first. And it turns out to be the biggest battle Henry has ever faced.

FEUD ALONG THE DEARBORN

Will DuRey

Until the night of the fire, Stanton, Montana, was a peaceful town. Its marshal, Silas Tasker, rejoiced in the knowledge that he had rid the town of the kind of rip-roaring reputation attributed to so many other cattle-towns across the west. But in the aftermath of the blaze that destroyed the barn on the Diamond-H ranch, a man lost his sanity, others died, and Silas found himself confronted with a feud capable of developing into an unstoppable range-war.